David Clifford Grieser was reared by loving parents on an Indian reservation in South Dakota. He earned his bachelor's degree at South Dakota State University and his master's at the University of South Dakota. After teaching English and directing all speech activities at the secondary level, he joined public television to facilitate the use of instructional television in classrooms in Iowa, Minnesota, and Wisconsin and ultimately became a trainer for an insurance company. Grieser is the author of *Survival on the Rosebud Indian Reservation* and currently is a freelance writer of his preferred medium: the short story.

To Jude.

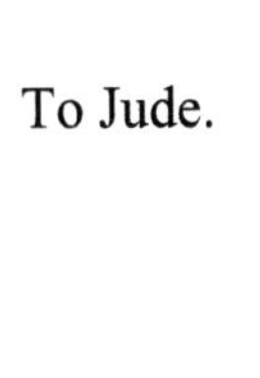

David Clifford Grieser

A Stab in the Heartland

AUSTIN MACAULEY PUBLISHERS™
LONDON • CAMBRIDGE • NEW YORK • SHARJAH

This is a work of fiction. Names, characters, businesses, places, events, locales, and incidents are either the products of the author's imagination or used in a fictitious manner. Any resemblance to actual persons, living or dead, or actual events is purely coincidental.

Ordering Information
Quantity sales: Special discounts are available on quantity purchases by corporations, associations, and others. For details, contact the publisher at the address below.

Publisher's Cataloging-in-Publication data
Grieser, David Clifford
A Stab in the Heartland

ISBN 9798889108313 (Paperback)
ISBN 9798889108320 (ePub e-book)

Library of Congress Control Number: 2024900004

www.austinmacauley.com/us

First Published 2024
Austin Macauley Publishers LLC
40 Wall Street, 33rd Floor, Suite 3302
New York, NY
USA

mail-usa@austinmacauley.com
+1 (646) 5125767

Thank you to everyone who influenced, supported, and motivated my writing to create this book.

Table of Contents

Payload

Sara wasn't looking for a boyfriend. After all, she was already engaged. And Gordon certainly didn't feel the need to find another girlfriend. He was comfortable with the few he could call, sometimes with short notices. The two of them were graduate students in Business Administration. Unlike undergraduate classes, those for masters' degrees were small, and their students had opportunities which at least afforded them probabilities that they would get to know one another by name, and at most, by addresses and phone numbers. It was little wonder, then, that Gordon and Sara first shared thoughts on balance sheets and later on bed sheets.

Working toward their MBAs, those two students had more in common than active libidos. They both had thirst for money.

Sara and Gordon were dedicated to their success. They spent hours developing problem-solving skills based upon actual Fortune 500 companies and establishing faux start-up ones to practice those skills in ways which could guide their own business decisions.

After classes they spent hours developing interpersonal and sexual skills which would guide their decision whether to share an apartment.

By the end of the fall semester, they found a one-bedroom apartment four blocks from campus. They notified existing landlords of their intentions to vacate the rooms, and Sara and Gordon began blissful cohabitation.

Phone calls between Sara and the man who thought he would be her husband had gone from infrequent to nearly nonexistent, and when he questioned the seriousness of their relationship, she replied, "We need more time apart," and broke the engagement.

Gordon simply stopped calling the women he had dated.

"We need to evaluate the risks we face with these companies," Sara told Gordon when they returned to classes.

Gordon argued that the risks should be considered on a continuum. "We don't necessarily have to eliminate them. Maybe we simply need to minimize those risks."

Being the detail-oriented individuals they had become, the two grad students applied the evaluation and minimization of risk to their personal lives: sexually transmitted diseases, pregnancy, bank accounts, buying groceries, restaurants, and entertainment.

"You think we should marry one another?" Sara asked.

"Sure. Why not?" Gordon answered. "Would you keep your last name or change it to mine? Sara Mehr has a nice ring to it."

"I don't know. For a quarter of a century, I've been accustomed to the last name of Knight."

"You could have a hyphenated name."

She retained her name when they eloped a month later. "Just minimizing risks," she explained.

By the end of the spring semester both Gordon and Sara had earned their masters' degrees in Business Administration, had traveled to Des Moines, Iowa, for job interviews, and had been offered positions there with life insurance companies, he at Principal and she at Nationwide.

Moving to Des Moines was the embodiment of the kind of life they sought. It meant money, lots of it. Gordon's success at Principal grew from his ability to motivate employees to perform at their best, and Sara was rewarded for assisting Nationwide with identifying the company's values and aligning business decisions with them.

After fourteen months of renting a loft in downtown Des Moines, they bought it, two bedrooms on the second floor overlooking the busy traffic on Ingersoll Avenue. They were considered good risks for credit. They bought new furniture. They leased new vehicles. They bought a gas grill for their deck. They paid cash for art for their new home.

It would be improbable that one employed by a life insurance company would not be aware of the benefits of life insurance, its ability to replace lost income in cases of death, in particular. Sara could not maintain her lifestyle with only her compensation, and Gordon needed her income in addition to his to retain the comfort to which they both had become accustomed. As a result, they bought life insurance from their respective companies, twenty-year term policies, each with a face-amount of one million dollars. Sara was the owner and payor for Gordon's policy, and Gordon owned and paid for Sara's. Should one of them die prematurely, the million dollars could be invested to provide the lost income.

There were other decisions, mostly economic, which they made. For example, they would not have children. They were too expensive. "Are we that selfish?" Gordon asked.

Without hesitating, Sara answered, "Without a doubt."

Gordon acquired a taste for bourbon and kept a cabinet stocked well enough that he could enjoy a daily drink or two after returning from work.

Additional time which the two of them worked meant less time together and fewer opportunities to make love. How long had it been now, a month? They did not care. Dollars were more important.

If there had existed at least some common interest in something other than money and sex, or if they had agreed to develop one, there would be a strong possibility that they could remain happily married after losing either one of those interests. It was the sexual intercourse which vanished.

The income remained a constant, but it was not increasing, and Sara blamed Gordon for not accepting the additional responsibility for training new agents at Principal. Gordon placed the blame for the stagnant income on Sara for her role in not communicating Nationwide's vision statement to her prospects.

Innocent incidents became problems. "I never told you this before, Sara, but I really hate it when you squeeze the tube of toothpaste in the middle."

"Why don't you clean the mirror, yourself, after you floss your teeth?" Sara asked.

"The bath mat is absolutely soaked after you shower. Try drying your feet a little before you get out of the tub," Gordon suggested.

"You left the toilet seat up when you came from the bathroom last night."

"When we're grocery-shopping you're coupon-crazy," Gordon told her, "Even though we don't need to use any. By the time you find the coupon to save fifteen cents on chocolate syrup, the ice cream has melted."

"You think you own the remote, and you want to control everything," she said. "I don't know where it goes at night, but I have to get out of bed to shut off the television."

"Sara, you know that you can't resist a good bargain. Tell me, though: what are we going to do with two flag poles?"

"No one is able to hear the news when Gordon is present. You start complaining as soon as you detect an error in grammar."

"You can't throw away anything. You save everything. You still have the carnation which your fiancé gave you when he took you to your high school prom."

The culmination of the conflict may have been when Gordon forgot their bank's PIN, so that he could withdraw cash. "Gordon, it's our wedding date."

The passion was gone. Work was mundane. But Sara and Gordon, for financial reasons, remained in their loft. Money was the basis for every decision. Eventually they would sell the loft. Until that happened, they would split the mortgage payments and costs of utilities. And each maintained the life insurance policy of one million dollars on the other.

While together at times, they would stare at one another across the table. Without speaking, they projected a disdain that only those who formerly loved one another could detect. *I thought I knew you*, each wondered while fantasizing what horrific plans were forming within the brain of the other.

They would never learn what the other had planned, but each knew instinctively that the death of one would benefit the survivor, and they understood the unexpressed wish each had that the other somehow would die. Somehow, they could live together with the satisfaction that a fateful end would result in a payout of one million dollars.

The major barrier to the probability that a death could occur soon, however, was life expectancy. Both were young, and, had they not been healthy, neither one would have been approved for the life insurance in the first place. They studied the policies which they owned on one another. Suicide would be covered after the policy is in force two years, but what are the chances that either would revert to self-harm, especially considering that each experienced a type of thrill that a million dollars were in the future?

When Sara read that a claim resulting from an accident is paid at any time, she found ways to leave promotional materials of mountain climbing and auto racing on Gordon's desk. And brochures on gymnastics and horseback riding began appearing on hers. In addition, they found advertisements for base jumping, sky diving, surfing, scuba diving, and careers in pyrotechnics and left them in convenient places for the other to see. An unspoken assumption that one wanted the other dead permeated every activity.

Divorce? Never. They were in the marriage for the money, regardless how long it would take. Although Sara's death would please Gordon, he would never have any part in planning it. And in his heart, he knew that Sara, as much as she would relish his dying, could not take an active role in hastening it.

Sara, however, was the more suspicious, in a way similar to paranoia. Unlike a clinical diagnosis in which the individual is fearful of people, in general, however, her fear was directed at one person, Gordon, albeit just as irrational. She was certain that Gordon had been preparing ways to inject dangers into all her activities, and, unless she were proactive, he very well could succeed in creating her fatality.

Sara made her move on her commute home from Nationwide. It was getting dark. She went to her favorite hardware store to ask its manager, Carl, for a recommendation on an effective way to eliminate mice. "Well, Ms. Knight, we have some traps which are easy to set."

"Carl, I cringe at the thought of discarding a dead mouse. Do you have anything else, a poison, for example?"

"Come with me. I'll show you." Carl walked ahead of Sara to an aisle lined with mouse traps. At the end of it and on the highest shelf Carl retrieved a small can. "This is probably the most effective poison you'll ever find," and pointed out its contents. "See this? The active ingredient is strychnine. Be careful with it. I wouldn't recommend it if there are children around."

"No. No children. Just a rodent." Sara paid for the poison and moved toward the door.

"You want your receipt?"

"No, a receipt isn't necessary." She placed the can into a pocket within her purse.

From the hardware store to their loft in downtown Des Moines, Sara posed various strategies for Gordon's ingesting the poison. In food? In a beverage? And would she be the one to add it to whatever he would be consuming, or could he, thinking that it is something else, do it, himself? Since earning her MBA and joining a nationally known insurance company, Sara gave less thought to ethics and personal consequences than to the most expeditious means to meet her goals. So, it was with her need to eliminate Gordon from her life. If she were not successful, he would be successful with her. "It's self-defense," she said aloud.

The second-story loft was unlit, so Gordon was not home. "As usual, working late," Sara whispered to herself. She ascended the stairway and entered a code to unlock the door. She switched on the light and hurried to the kitchen to find a knife to cut the plastic which covered the lid of the poison, and to find an opener to pry off the top. The substance, she discovered, consisted of granules, most likely attractive to a mouse, but obviously incongruent with a human diet, and she emptied them into a food processor to pulverize the tiny pellets into a fine powder. Sara then placed the powder in its original container, snapped on its lid, and dropped the can into her purse.

After rinsing the processor and putting it top down into the dishwasher, Sara filled the bath tub with soap and hot water, undressed, and leaned back into the tub to soak. The bubble bath became the agent to cleanse what would be the worst deed she ever would perpetrate, and she imagined the evil sliding down the drain, just as the dishwasher would carry away all traces of the poison. She lay in the tub and thought, *Maybe the dishwasher would not eliminate all the traces of poison. Carl, after all, indicated how toxic it is.*

Sara stood, grabbed a towel, quickly patted herself dry, slipped into her bath robe, and scurried into the kitchen. She opened the door of the washer and looked at the inverted food processor. There probably were remnants of the poison on it, just as there sometimes are leftover marks from soap.

"Remnants," she said aloud. She went to the cupboard to retrieve one of two Old Fashioned glasses which Gordon characteristically used for his bourbon. From her purse she pulled the can of poison, pried off the lid, and dusted the bottom of the glass with it. She then added a few drops of water to make a thin paste and swirled the glass until a dull whiteness thinly coated the inside of the glass almost half-way to the top. She then took the glass into the bathroom to get her hair dryer. Sara turned the blow dryer onto the glass to eliminate any remaining moisture, returned the glass to the cupboard, replaced the lid on the poison, and let the can fall back into her purse.

Sara's freedom that evening was about to end. At first, she heard footsteps approaching the door and then the light tapping of numbers on the key-less entry pad. Gordon entered. They looked at one another only briefly, but expressionless.

"Hi," Sara said, slightly more exuberant than she normally would address him.

Gordon responded with, "Yeah." He immediately strode to his liquor cabinet, clinched the bottle of bourbon by its neck, and set it on the kitchen counter. He pulled open the cupboard door, pulled the highball glass from the shelf, and placed it next to the liquor.

"Maybe I'll also have one," Sara said as she watched Gordon's daily ritual. It was almost as though she were relishing what was to occur, without sharing his aberration for their relationship. If she ever needed a drink, though, it was then.

Responding to Sara, he took down the other glass. As he was about to pour the whiskey into his glass, he made an observation to Sara. "This glass appears not to have been cleaned very well."

"Oh, it's clean," Sara replied, "But I had used the last of the *Rinse Stain Remover*, so there are some water marks on it."

Gordon poured the bourbon into each glass until they were half full, an event of which an optimist could take note. "I really need to shower," he said.

"Wait. I'll empty the tub," Sara replied. "I started a bubble bath, but got out when you came home." She left Gordon and entered the bathroom, and during the thirty seconds that she was away from the kitchen, Gordon noticed that, although his glass contained water marks, hers did not. *Not very appetizing*, he thought. *Considering that she feels that it is all right to drink out of a glass with residue, maybe she should have the one with the marks on it*, and he replaced her glass with his.

Sara returned to the kitchen. While she sipped her bourbon, Gordon drained his, and then poured a few ounces more into his glass. The two of them sat in silence until Gordon noticed that Sara winced. "What's wrong?"

"I don't know."

He shrugged, finished his bourbon, and started toward the bathroom.

Sara began shaking. She stood and then placed her hands and knees on the floor. Gordon turned to look at her. Sara moaned, turned over on her side, and began wildly moving her arms and legs. Her robe opened. The convulsions worsened, and she clutched her throat. Breathing was difficult.

Gordon grabbed his phone and pressed 911. Within a few seconds he tried to answer questions. First, he provided his address. Then he tried to follow advice. "No, I can't do anything…She can't talk…She's twitching all over…I don't think she's breathing…OK."

Sara's muscles relaxed. Her mouth opened, and a white foam spilled out of it. She was motionless, her eyes wide open. By the time the paramedics had reached Sara, she was dead. The medical technicians took the gurney from the ambulance and wheeled the lifeless Sara into the truck, and two police officers, one a young man and the other a female sergeant, arrived to question Gordon.

Gordon knew nothing. Sara seemed fine when he entered their loft. Did Gordon want to harm his wife for any reason? Had he ever threatened her? Was he seeing someone else? Was *she* seeing anyone else? How did they feel about their jobs? Were there marital difficulties? Financial problems?

The detectives asked Gordon if he would allow them to look around the house. "Of course, you may. I, too, want to know what happened. I was home only long enough to drink some bourbon with her."

They began opening cupboards and closet doors, and next they pulled on latex gloves. The sergeant pointed at the highball glasses. "Are those the glasses you used for the bourbon?"

"Yes."

"We'd like to take these with us. We'll return them if the lab doesn't find anything." The sergeant carefully placed the glasses into two sturdy containers and then spotted Sara's purse. In it she found the canister holding the mouse poison. "Do you have a problem with mice in your house?"

"No. Never."

"Can you explain why, then, your wife had mouse poison in her purse?"

"No, I cannot. I had never seen it until now."

The sergeant placed the can in separate plastic, and called to the male officer, "Detective Royce, have you found anything else? If not, I think we can go now. I'm leaving my business card with you, Mr. Mehr. If you learn anything more, or if you have questions, please call me."

Gordon had no reason to call the officers. He would know nothing more than he did that night. The officers returned to their cruiser, and Gordon made a note to call the funeral home after the medical examiner was done with what he assumed would be an autopsy.

The officers, however, did not forget Gordon. They notified him that his wife's death was the result of strychnine poisoning and cautioned him to be available for questioning. "Do not travel more than fifty miles from metropolitan Des Moines," he was ordered.

What a strange predicament, he felt. *We may not have had the best of marriages, and I'm not that upset that she's out of my life*, he thought, *but murder*? It did not stop him, though, from taking advantage of Principal's practice of granting five days of leave for bereavement.

Gordon called the funeral home to indicate that it was his and Sara's wish for her to be cremated.

Most of the time during his leave, he remained in the loft, going through Sara's possessions. He chuckled when he saw some of the promotions for risky avocations, and he briefly reviewed each before stuffing it into the recycling bin. He stopped when he saw the feature on pyrotechnics. An advertisement next to it promised that its company could use cremated remains for a small rocket which would *explode in beautiful colors in the night sky*. Perfect, he felt. *What would he do with an urn full of ashes, anyway?*

Cremation commenced. Gordon received the urn. He packed the remains and sent them to the company which promised the sky rocket, and he announced to employees at Principal and Nationwide that a memorial service would take place at a later date.

The Des Moines Police Department also had been busy, with the case of Sara Knight. Officers canvassed stores which sold rat poisons. They kept with them photographs of Sara to show to owners, managers, and employees.

"That's Ms. Knight," Carl told a detective. "Sara Knight. Sure, I remember when she came in to buy it. Had a problem with mice, she said. She was a good customer. I'm really sorry to hear the bad news from you. Anything I can do?"

"No, you've been very helpful. Thank you."

The chief of police closed the case. The final report included in bold letters SUICIDE. Because the life insurance policy had not been in force for at least two years, there was no death benefit Gordon would receive. Instead, Principal returned to him all the premiums he had paid.

Gordon's household income was now half what it had been. The million-dollar payout was a pipe dream. He knew that the poison was meant for him, but there was solace: Sara, instead, had died.

Because federal laws do not allow deliveries of explosive devices via mail, a courier delivered Gordon's rocket. Happily, he noted that the skyrocket had an exceptionally long fuse. Initially, he had intended to launch the firework as part of a memorial service for the benefit of all Sara's colleagues at Nationwide and his at Principal. However, there was a cognitive dissonance between his perception of a memorial service, which inherently included mourning, and a celebration, which more appropriately described his mental state, similar to a Fourth of July event. Screw the public. He needed to do this on his own.

On a cool, but clear, evening Gordon drove to Clearwater Beach in West Des Moines with a man-made lake with imported sand and miles of shoreline without the glare of lights from houses or even automobiles. He had the rocket fueled with Sara's remains and a butane lighter he had bought for the gas grill. He lifted the rocket from the trunk of his car and planted it strategically between a bike path and the shoreline and aimed it over the water.

Should he say a prayer? He didn't know. He was happy that he had survived, but sad that he had received nothing from the disaster. He lost both a household income and a million dollars in proceeds. "Stuff happens," he said under his breath and lit the fuse. He then hurried to his car to witness the lift-off.

He watched the burning fuse. When it reached the bottom of the rocket, the sparks stopped. Nothing happened. He waited, perhaps half a minute, and the rocket still did not launch. He sat, glaring through the front windshield. *Not seeing what is left of Sara soaring into the sky can't be her ultimate revenge*, he thought. He waited longer, enough time to contemplate his and her academic success, their careers, and even their crumbled marriage.

No, her ultimate revenge had to be her denying him the million dollars from the insurance policy for which he had paid. He approached the rocket. Should he return it to the manufacturer? Should he attempt to relight it?

Gordon bent over the dormant rocket. Sara's revenge, it seemed, was not that she had kept him from getting a million dollars or that she denied him the pleasure of watching her light up the sky, but that he had not waited long enough for the rocket to launch. The skyrocket ignited, and Gordon's head, directly above it, kept it from ascending. It did not, however, prevent it from exploding.

A young woman, running on the bike path early the next morning, saw the body.

"It looks as though death was instantaneous," the coroner remarked to the two police officers who had summoned him.

One of the officers answered, "At least he didn't suffer."

What did they know?

The Lake Effect

Why do some people have unremarkable lives, Mortimer Novotny thought as the last of his employees left his grocery store for the first weekend in October, *and others are filled with excitement?* The greatest elation which had ever characterized his life probably resulted from successful weekend sales at Novotny's Groceries. His father, Edward Novotny, began selling fruits, vegetables, and canned goods half a century ago in Duluth, Minnesota, and Mortimer worked in the store as a teenager. When Ed died a few years later, his widow wanted no part of the business, and their only child inherited it.

It seemed that Mortimer experienced more satisfaction from his store than he did from his marriage to Ethel, whom he married after adding a walk-in freezer to Novotny's. The two never had children. "Poor Mort has a low sperm count," she told her friends, although there was no medical evidence to support the statement. Mortimer had the store before he had Ethel, and he claimed to have the best produce in town.

The young men and women who worked for Mortimer often referred to him as *Mr. Monotony* but not so he could hear them. There were times that someone mistakenly would address him as "monotony," and Mortimer would hear "Novotny."

Have I ever initiated anything positive in my life? he wondered. *I didn't even start my own store. Even "Mortimer" is a boring name.*

Novotny's Groceries was located just off Mesaba Avenue in downtown Duluth. Mortimer turned off the lights, ambled to the front door, and turned around the sign which hung from the inside of the door and which had OPEN printed on one side and CLOSED on the other. He stepped outside, locked the door, and went to his car, waiting for him at one of the spaces for employees.

It was snowing. Snow was far from unusual in Duluth. And when it arrived, it stayed until late spring. Mortimer kept a pair of boots in his car permanently. He remembered when the Fourth of July celebration was cancelled as a result of sleet. Generally cold weather was more common than warm in Duluth, but the city's temperatures were usually different from those in cities farther from Lake Superior. The *lake effect* tended to keep temperatures far above normal during winters in Duluth and much colder during summers.

I need to do something exciting, he mused, as he drove onto Mesaba. He had no hobbies, nothing to provide respite to ordering goods, stocking shelves, and doing payrolls, and no alternative to an obedience which Ethel demanded. His only close friend, Arnie, who lived alone in the same condominium complex, but on the third floor, had a pilot's license. *And I don't know how to operate anything but an old Buick with an automatic transmission.*

Mortimer cruised along Mesaba until it joined East Skyline Parkway, where he turned.

Arnie had taken Mort up in his plane a few times for an aerial view of Duluth, the harbor, and Lake Superior, and, as much as Mortimer enjoyed the flights, earning a license to fly was not an avocation in which he wanted to invest too many resources. *Skydiving probably wouldn't require much training*, he said to himself, *but I don't know if I'm brave enough.*

It was snowing more heavily, and Mortimer knew it would continue most of the night. *The weather is terrible to be in a small airplane. How can I even think of jumping out of one? I need to hold that thought until spring.*

East Skyline merged into Kenwood Avenue. It was in the Kenwood area where he and Ethel owned a condominium on the second floor with a deck attached to the west side. Mortimer drove to his single-car garage close to the middle of twenty-eight others, attached to one another end to end, all identical, except the number on each one, which corresponded to the number on the door of each condo, Number 13 for him. He pressed a battery-operated opener, and the door lifted to allow him to drive in. He reached over the seat to get his boots and exchanged his shoes for them. Mortimer took the remote opener with him to close the door and ascended a stairway to Number 13.

As he turned the door knob, he heard the shout of Ethel, "I just cleaned the floor. Take off your shoes and leave them in the hallway. I don't want a mess." Mortimer did as he was told.

Mortimer always did as he was told, not liking it, but accepting it. He opened the door, which pushed a throw rug across the wood floor of the living room and dining area. He removed his gloves and coat, placed them in the coat closet, and, without speaking or looking at Ethel, moved to the table and sat. Ethel placed a crock pot full of split-pea soup between them. "I made split-pea soup," she said.

"Oh," answered Mortimer. He remembered when they would kiss one another when he returned from work, even if one of them were not happy with the other. So did she. At some time during their eight years of marriage, however, they stopped. Neither was happy with the other, but neither was unhappy, either. The prevailing mood was, *this is the way things are.*

Ethel and Mortimer ate in silence and, when finished, stood up almost in unison to take their bowls to the kitchen. He then unfolded the Duluth *Herald* and took it with him to a chair to read while Ethel removed from the dryer clean clothing to fold.

The Novotny couple had two bedrooms, one for each of them, because Ethel had complained a few years ago that Mortimer snored. When he finished reading the paper, he showered, went directly to his room, turned down the blankets, and lay on his pink sheets, which she had bought for both beds.

Fantasizing about skydiving kept Mortimer awake for hours. *Would I ever be able to complete an activity which could even remotely be considered heroic?* He resolved to answer that question by exploring possibilities the next day.

If not removed, snow in Duluth will remain for months, and the accumulated weight jeopardizes structures. One often shovels snow from his roof, for example. In the morning Mortimer went to the sliding glass door to the deck and pulled back a curtain. The snow was high enough to cover the redwood chaise lounge. Instead of shaving and showering, Mortimer was primarily concerned with removing the snow, and he grabbed his coat and gloves, retrieved the boots he had left outside the door the night before, and trudged to the garage for the shovel. He returned to the condo and cradled his boots as he crossed the room to the deck. Once outside, Mortimer pushed the top snow off the deck until he could lift shovels full. When he had cleared an area that allowed him to peer over the railing, he marveled at the depth of the snow below.

"Hey, Mortie," yelled a ten-year-old playmate of Mortimer. They were the same age, and both thrived on winter activities. They were on a berm at the edge of the playground at Lester Park Elementary School, and the snow bank was level with their feet. "Let's see who can jump the farthest into that snow." They jumped. They argued who won, but neither cared. Mortimer simply remembered the thrill.

If I can't jump into that snow drift below, there's no way that I can skydive, Mortimer scolded himself. He stretched his legs over the top, held onto the railing behind him, leaned forward, and released his grip. He plunged nearly two feet into the four-foot bank, and, for an instant, he was Mortie at Lester Park. It was *deja vu*.

Mortimer dug himself out, returned the shovel, and, removing his boots, re-entered his home. Ethel was making coffee in the kitchen. "Where were you?"

"Clearing snow. I'm going to do more."

After the warmth of half a cup, he left. Instead of going outside, however, he darted down the hall to a stairway which would take him to the third floor, where Arnie lived. Mortimer was almost exuberant as he described his goal to skydive and how he was acclimating himself to the feeling of weightlessness. "You really jumped off your deck?"

"Sure did," Mortimer answered, "but I'm looking for more height," and convinced Arnie to let him jump from his, one story higher. The snow cushioned his fall just as well as that under his deck had.

Among twenty-eight condominium owners, it would be unlikely that at least one individual would not have seen a man flailing his arms and legs as he dropped from a deck into the snow below it. Ethel heard from concerned neighbors and confronted Mortimer. "What do you think you're doing?"

"Trying to have fun."

"You must have looked ridiculous. Stop embarrassing me. I mean it."

At that point Mortimer felt obligated to explain why he had done such things.

Ethel was even more livid when Mortimer introduced the word *skydive*. "You will do no such thing. Don't you ever even think about it."

As he had done in the past, Mortimer did as he was told. He would not skydive. But he loved the rush he felt during the freefall, and he knew that Arnie could help him.

"Sure, you could jump from my plane into snow. It's been done, but you'll need much more than a four- or five-foot bank. And you'll need better insulated clothing and gloves. And don't forget goggles and a face mask." Although Arnie chose his remarks for the purpose of dissuading Mort, his admonitions actually created the blueprint for his carrying out his mission. What was worse, though, is that Arnie was convincing himself that Mort could do it.

Residents of northern Minnesota, in general, and Duluth, in particular, considered themselves a tough breed. Schools and businesses rarely closed during snow storms. Most of the blizzards came from the west, and anyone could withstand them. Those which came from the east, over Lake Superior, however, were the most feared, and even the simplest of meteorologists' predictions of a storm from the east were enough to convince school administrators and merchants to close their doors early and send the kids and employees home.

As Arnie and Mort anticipated, snow storms continued from the west. They must wait for an eastward storm to create the snow whose depth could break a fall from an airplane.

The storm for which Mort and Arnie were waiting, one from the east, occurred during the first week of February. When Duluthians heard it was coming, they emptied store shelves of bottled water and non-perishable foods. They bought kerosene lamps and gasoline generators. They purchased additional blankets. And they went to their homes hours ahead of the impending storm. They were ready. So were Mort and Arnie.

The blizzard from the Lake hit the Duluth area as an uncontrollable wild fire could consume the Superior National Forest. It touched everything.

When the storm had passed there were the constant sounds of gasoline engines, some propelling snow blowers and others fueling snowmobiles. Some of the drifts in the West End were as high as second-floor windows.

For Arnie and Mort, the waiting was almost over. They needed only sunshine. It would be another three days, and the new sound of an engine was Arnie's airplane. Mort was with him, with thickly insulated clothing, heavy boots, and goggles. Arnie brought with him a pair of flares.

They soared over Lake Superior, over the city of Superior at the tip of the lake in Wisconsin, over the ships which had been docked for days in the harbor, and over the aerial lift bridge, which opened to allow the largest vessels to enter. They flew northeast along the lakeshore. They were searching for what they considered pristine snow, white as a cloud on a summer's day.

The entire landscape appeared bright white.

Once Arnie reached the city of Lakewood along the shore, he decided to get farther from Lake Superior and turned the plane west. Within 15 minutes, he could see below him an oval area tilting from the southwest to the northeast, a vast area of pure whiteness. "Look at that," he said to Mort and pointed. "There must be two thousand acres of snow down there."

"Nice. I'm ready." Mort pulled on his goggles.

Arnie circled the oval. "When you say *go*, I'll fly over the center of it. We should be really close to Highway 4. Use the flares, so I can find you quickly."

This is it, he thought. *If I fail to do this, I never will do it.* "Go."

Arnie banked to the right, and Mort pushed open the door. The cold filled the cabin instantly, and Arnie clinched his teeth. It seemed that the iron grip he had on the steering gear was a pair of frozen hands.

Mortimer let his body be pulled from the plane, and Arnie quickly latched the door.

It was a drop of only a few hundred feet, but for the first time in his life, Mortimer felt as though he had reached a milestone which few had achieved. In addition, he experienced a sense of freedom that had been missing since his marriage to Edith. And, what's more, it was a sunny day, which allowed him an unrestrictive view of the environment, his environment. *I don't even have to experience the anxieties about whether a parachute could fail to open,* he thought.

Mortimer looked below him. There was movement across part of that lovely-looking oval, a steady orchestration of action from what appeared to be—what were they—children? He continued the descent, thirty-two feet per second, squared. They were skating. Then he knew. "Ice!" he screamed.

Jack and Jill

It began with a "Hi" from Mr. John Piersen, a teacher at Brookings High School. It was the month of June, and John was enrolled in education classes at South Dakota State University.

Jill Jannsen responded, "Hello." She, too, aspired to teach, and she had been reading notes which students had tacked to a bulletin board in the Education Department when John approached.

"Are you starting classes this summer?" he asked, knowing that there was no other reason for her being there.

"Yes, I need to take the Gifted and Talented class before I can be accepted into supervised student teaching."

"You're a senior, then?"

"Yes," she replied. "You?"

"I graduated a year ago and accepted my first teaching assignment here in Brookings. Once I earn an additional fifteen semester hours, I'm to get a ten-percent pay increase, so I started graduate school this summer. I'm Jack," he said. Jack was no more than five feet, seven inches tall, but he exuded a confidence which Jill noted quickly, and he was thin, but his broad shoulders gave him an athletic appearance. It was his dark blue eyes, though, which captured most of her attention.

"I'm Jill." She grinned. Maybe it was her perfectly spaced white teeth that made him want to remain in front of the bulletin board with her. Her five-foot-three, slender frame suggested to him that healthful diets were important to her. *Maybe she is even a vegetarian*, he thought.

"Maybe we'll see one another again." Jack could not think of anything else to say.

"Yeah, maybe. Nice meeting you, Jack."

They shook hands, and Jack continued to keep his hand around hers. "Could I call you sometime?" They pulled out their cell phones, exchanged numbers, and shook hands once more. "I'm Jack *Piersen*," he said.

"My last name is *Jannsen*," Jill told him.

For two days Jack ignored the urge to call, out of fear that Jill would consider him too assertive. His limit, though, was three days, and he called to ask whether she might be interested in going with him to a conference on the role of active listening in counseling couples. It would be Friday evening at seven in the Student Union.

"Sure." She had hoped that he would call. "I'll meet you there."

That Friday, a moderator summarized the Rogers and Far son paper on which active listening is based and introduced a panel of counselors. Both Jill and Jack would later describe the summary as *enlightening*, but happy that they left when the experts began discussing its shortcomings in marriage counseling.

As they walked to the dormitory where Jill was staying, they learned that their lives were stark contrasts. Jill had come from northern Minnesota. In summers, she would swim and water ski, and during winters it was down-hill skiing and ice skating. Hockey was her favorite spectator sport. Jack had lived on the Rosebud Indian Reservation in south central South Dakota, and his pastimes consisted of hiking and exploring hills and caves.

"Are you Indian?" Jill asked.

"No, my parents worked for the Public Health Service hospital. They weren't my biological parents. I never knew my mother and father. I always had a foster home. You know those ancestry tests? The ones that use saliva to find genetic relatives? I had one done. I get reports fairly often. I guess I hoped that there would be a name which someday would identify one of my parents."

Jill smiled. "Wow. I also grew up in foster homes, but I never considered trying to find my real parents."

Jack continued. "The chances that I find them are probably one in over a million. You see, my biological mom or dad would have to have used the same ancestry lab that I used. There are many companies which do it, and if they decided to use one, and it happened to be different from mine, I would never know. Even if I never find them, though, I've learned a lot about where around the world my ancestors lived and moved. You would enjoy reading the results. They'll tell you how many genes you have in common with people you've never even heard of. The only address and phone number I can give you, though, is the one I used, but it's accurate."

Their sharing the experiences of adapting to new sets of parents and adjusting to different sisters and brothers represented what seemed to be their only common characteristic, but it created a bond which resulted in a friendship which neither would ever want to lose. It also served as the basis for discussions of the stability of relationships involving foster children. For example, would they develop effective parenting skills? *Could* they?

Jill and Jack saw one another almost daily. If they were unable to meet for lunch or watch movies at Jack's apartment, they called between classes. Kisses and hugs were transformed into petting and foreplay, and by the end of June they had had sexual intercourse.

Classes ended after a sultry July. Jill relinquished her dorm room, and Jack invited her to live with him. In August, three weeks before schools would begin, Jill announced, "I'm pregnant," something for which one can never be fully prepared.

Their own mothers had given them up for adoption, and Jack could not imagine his own son or daughter in one or more foster homes. In addition, their biological mothers never married. When a child's parents are married to one another, he had read, they are less likely to separate.

"Marriage would be best for our child," he told Jill, "and I think terrific for us." They went to the court house for a marriage license, found a Justice of the Peace to perform the wedding ceremony, chose wedding bands, and were married by the end of the month. After the wedding vows, the Justice of the Peace looked intently at both of them and remarked, "You're going to have good-looking kids."

They did not *have to* get married, they told each other; they *wanted to*.

Mr. Piersen began his second year of teaching with new goals, most of them associated with a wife and an eventual child, and Ms. Jannsen-Piersen began her supervised student teaching in the Brookings Middle School. She would be certified to teach by the end of the academic year.

When Jack initially met Jill, he imagined her as someone dedicated to good health, and the way in which she was preparing for childbirth confirmed it. Healthful foods, exercise, and sound sleeping were the norm, and Jill kept regular appointments with her gynecologist. She would nurse the baby.

What would they name their child? A baby girl would be *Agatha Jannsen*, and a boy would have the name of *Owen Piersen*.

By January an ultrasound confirmed that they would have a boy.

"Wouldn't it be nice if Owen could have grandparents who, against our best judgement, would spoil him?" She was looking at Jack. Then she looked away and said to herself, "Everyone should have a grandma and grandpa." After considering her declaration Jill retrieved her things-to-do-someday file and found the phone number which Jack had given her for the ancestry lab. Within seven minutes Jill had ordered the kit and paid for it. It would be shipped the next day.

"The chances aren't good that you'll find either of them," Jack reminded her, "but it provides great entertainment."

The test kit arrived days later, although Jill was too busy with her assignments at the middle school to open it, and Jack had preparations for his history classes and papers to correct, and gave no thought to it until spring break in March. It was during the five days which they had all to themselves that they again addressed the subject of grandparents, and Jill opened the test kit. Embarrassed over how simple the instructions were, she filled a small tube with her saliva, sealed it in the self-addressed, postage-paid envelope, and walked it directly to the postal collection box in front of the apartment complex. *Why had she not done it sooner?* she asked herself.

Jill earned her degree in May from S. D. S. U. and began searching locally for schools which needed teachers in September. Jack completed his second year in May at Brookings High School, signed a contract to begin his third year of teaching in September, and enrolled in graduate classes for a second summer.

May also was the month for the birth of Owen. Contractions began during the three weeks separating the end of the school year from the beginning of summer school, and, as Jack drove her to the Brookings Municipal Hospital, Jill, considering the perfect timing, exclaimed, "The gods are with us."

Jack told a receptionist that his wife was having contractions a minute apart, and a nurse had a wheel chair to transport her from the car to the maternity ward. "We'll let you know when we are all done."

It was getting dark, and Jack sat alone in Waiting Room Number 1. Hours went by. The receptionist had left for the evening. He stood and looked around the room. *Where is everyone?* he asked himself. He wanted to find someone who knew Jill's condition. There was no one. He returned to a chair and sat. He was tired. He began sleeping a few minutes at a time. "Mr. Pierson," a nurse startled him. "You can see your wife now. It was a difficult delivery. The doctor will be in to talk with you."

Jill appeared to be sleeping when Jack entered her room, but she knew the moment he was next to her. "I want to see my baby," she said to the walls and ceiling.

"Mr. and Mrs. Piersen," Dr. Sukara began, "We had some problems."

"I want to see him," Jill responded. "Don't you usually let the mother hold her baby?"

"We wanted to run some tests first," the doctor said. "He has an elongated skull and a cleft palate. We can correct a cleft palate with surgery, but there are other characteristics which, if problematic, we have no way to fix. We feel that he has a depleted immune system, which means he will have a difficult time fighting infections, even the common cold. In addition, we are certain that he will suffer from severe intellectual deficits." A nurse brought in Owen, wrapped in a blanket, and placed him in Jill's arms. "I'm sorry," Dr. Sukara lamented, and left.

Two days later on a Friday Jill went home with Jack. The ancestry test had arrived with Jill's DNA. "Who cares? What grandparents would even want to see Owen now?" Jill addressed Jack. They returned Sunday to prepare to take Owen home and to get instructions on how to care for him properly.

It was a fitful night between Sunday and Monday. Owen awoke nearly every hour, and Jill could not nurse him. Instead, she used a bottle which allowed her to let the baby formula drip into his mouth. He was sleeping when Jill and Jack sat together on the sofa. Jill opened her ancestry results. Her ancestors were mainly from northern Europe.

There was a list of names of individuals with whom she shared genes, names of which she had never heard, percentages generally ranging from .015 percent to 3.6 percent. Jack followed the list, continued on a second page. His name was on it: John Piersen. Shared genes: 50 percent. They were brother and sister.

When it concerns characters and circumstances, a writer is omnipotent, so he or she can do anything at all within the story. I could have told you what Jack and Jill did next, how they reacted to discovering that they had the same mother. Had either of them even suspected that they were related, the relationship would have taken a different course. If Jack had known about Jill's genes, for example, he would not have got into her jeans. And I could have written exactly what they did with Owen, but I thought it would be more interesting if I left it up to you, the reader. Whatever you think happened to Jack, Jill probably came tumbling after.

Sharing a Body

She sat in the last desk in the second row from the window in what was known as the *home room* and Loren tried to steel glances at her when she was not looking at him. But she always knew when anyone stared. She had two names, Sheila and Tiffany, because she was really two individuals. She did not have a dissociative personality disorder. She literally had two personalities.

Sheila and Tiffany were to be identical twins, but they did not completely separate before birth. Obstetricians offered surgery which would result in one girl who would be normal, but their parents objected. It would mean the death of the other. The conjoined girls, then, matured as their peers did.

Shock at first sight was always the response from others. In time, however, everyone became accustomed to two heads on one body.

Loren had always felt an outsider among his classmates. Throughout elementary school he had been part of schoolmates' birthday parties only when the entire class had been invited. Now a senior in high school, he had never dated a girl and had no close friends. *If anyone should feel ostracized*, he thought, *it should be Sheila and Tiffany*. But those girls had a warmth about them that made others want to be with them, and it was the likely reason that Loren was so attracted to the two.

After a teacher took the daily lunch count, students were ready for their first classes.

"Hi, Sheila," Loren murmured.

"Hello, Loren," Sheila replied. "My sister's here, too. 'I'm sorry', Tiffany. I was really talking to both of you. Would it be alright if I sat with you for lunch today?"

"Their eyes turned to one another, and Sheila shrugged her shoulder. 'Okay'," Tiffany said.

Three classes separated him from what seemed would be the closest thing to a date which he had ever had. His English class seemed to drag. Shakespeare's *McBeth* led him to consider that Sheila and Tiffany could easily plot against him, that they were as evil as Lady McBeth.

Loren's class in economics bored him. The subject was microeconomics, including household budgets, and he mused about the house in which Sheila and Tiffany lived. *How many were even in their home? Did the annual census count them as one or two?*

His last class before lunch was Drivers' Education. Sheila and Tiffany drove. *Did they need one or two drivers' licenses?* He would ask them.

The twins saved Loren a seat across from them. When he sat, the students next to him moved to another table. "We each have a driver's license," Tiffany told him, "but I earned a higher score than Sheila." They shared a lower spine and everything below it. Sheila controlled the left arm, and Tiffany the right, and coordination was a top priority in a car.

Lunch consisted of pizza, garlic bread, green beans, and a peanut butter cookie. Sheila ate the pizza and bread. Tiffany devoured the cookie and said, "I don't care much for beans."

"What? You have the same stomach," Loren remarked.

"So? We have our own taste buds," was the answer from Tiffany.

They had their own lungs, and sometimes one would catch a cold or have a fever without affecting the other.

Each had her own heart, and one could have a faster pulse than the other simply as a result of different responses to outside stimuli: movies (they would buy two tickets), airplanes (they could purchase one seat), and thunderstorms (one of them may wake up while the other slept). Loren wondered whether one of them could like him at the same time that the other did not. He was learning, for example, that their tastes differed in ways other than foods. Sheila seemed more reserved, whereas Tiffany relished new experiences. *Maybe Sheila and Tiffany were incarnations of a conflict which afflicts everyone*, he thought.

"Could we do this again?" Loren referred to having lunch.

Sheila and Tiffany actually enjoyed explaining to Loren their relationship. They answered questions which others had, but would not ask. And Loren could not get enough of them. Not only did he delight in learning what they had in common and private, but also, he felt, regardless of how accurate it may be, that they liked him.

In addition to having frequent lunches together, they often studied together after school.

Toward the end of the academic year, Loren, after practicing a monologue in front of his bedroom mirror, asked Sheila and Tiffany if they could be interested in seeing a movie with him Saturday evening. *The Fault in Our Stars* was playing at the Orpheum, and Loren would pay for their tickets. "Yes," they decided, and considering that Loren did not yet have his driver's license, announced, "We'll pick you up thirty minutes before the show starts."

The conjoined sisters preferred to sit toward the back of a theatre, where they were less likely to block the sight of patrons behind them, and, after paying for three tickets, Loren followed them into a back row of seats. *Sheila and Tiffany seem to be pretty normal*, he thought. *And both of them like popcorn.* The movie was, in fact, a romantic one, and when he noticed tears in Tiffany's eyes, he let his left hand touch her right. To his astonishment, she held his hand in hers, and Loren was not about to let go, unless he were forced to do it. The movie ended without Sheila's knowing that there was any hand-holding. *I sat beside the right girl*, he thought. *Sheila didn't even appear to be sad.*

When the girls drove Loren home, he hesitated to open the door, and, instead, turned to give Tiffany a hug. As he placed his left arm on her shoulder, she turned and kissed him on the mouth. It was the first time for him, a milestone, an event which he would always treasure. Then he faced a dilemma. *How could I show affection for Tiffany without giving the same attention to Sheila?* To compensate for the disparity, Loren stretched his right arm across both of them, so that his hand rested on Sheila's left shoulder and approached her face with his. Sheila abruptly turned her head away from him.

Loren's night ended, then, with both a love for Tiffany and a snub from Sheila. *What will happen now? With an omnipresent Sheila, will Tiffany ever want to be with me again?*

He had his answer before the next weekend. "Yes, we'll go with you to another movie." Again, he sat to the right of Tiffany and this time held her hand through most of the film. And when they drove him home, without pretense, before opening the door, he embraced mostly Tiffany and placed his mouth on hers.

Soon they would be eliminating movies and, instead, be parking for nearly the same length of time that they sat in the theatre. And Sheila did not seem to mind. She let Tiffany do what she pleased. Even when Tiffany pulled Loren's hand under her bra, Sheila ignored it. *Tiffany could feel his hand on the right breast. Could Sheila?* So long as Sheila did not object, Loren did not care. *Sheila not only did not object, but also, she seemed to encourage Tiffany's behavior. What does Sheila get out of it?* he wondered.

The story of conjoined Sheila and Tiffany with Loren has a denouement. It began in the automobile when Tiffany pushed her hand into his underwear and felt his genitals. Intime, he did the same with hers, but suddenly confronted the realization that, because Sheila and Tiffany shared a vagina, Sheila also could feel what he was doing. And she let him do it. And she ignored him. *What did Sheila want?*

As would happen with any couple, maybe in this case, *couples*, the heavy petting morphed into sexual intercourse. They would exit the front seat, and Sheila and Tiffany would lie down in the back. Loren would pull off their panties, and Tiffany would guide Loren's penis into their vagina. Loren could tell that Tiffany liked it and that Sheila did not dislike it. In some ways he was having sex with two women at the same time. In other ways he felt there was an up-close voyeur who experienced more sexual satisfaction than a voyeur could ever get.

Sex with Tiffany-Sheila was something he anticipated with overflowing testosterone, but an act which left him void of the kind of privacy for which he yearned. Sheila literally was always over Tiffany's shoulder. Later Sheila began seeing less fornication, because Loren began seeing less of Tiffany.

Here is the denouement: Sheila and Tiffany were a type of outcast, and Loren was a different kind of outcast, a probable reason for their interests in one another.

Tiffany, sensual and impulsive, represented the instinctual part of a human being, and Sheila stood for the social and ethical standards which made large groups of people living together possible. The two of them acted against one another in the same way in which everyone confronts a two-sided decision. It was Yin and Yang.

Sheila, the more conservative one, never initiated sex. Tiffany did, and Sheila shared in the pleasure. Sheila could sort of say, then, that she was chaste.

Apparently, it worked well for both of them. When a man eventually proposed to Sheila, she accepted the engagement and eventually married him. Sheila had saved herself for her husband, and Tiffany could share in the rewards. And Tiffany would prove to be the better voyeur.

Revenge of a Cuckhold

Never mind that they met in a tavern on Court Avenue, so named as a result of the court house at the end of the street. That was two months ago. Samantha remained an interesting and enigmatic girl, and she found Daniel funny and charming.

During the beginning of their romance each of them devised scenarios that would result in their being together. Later, they felt no need to postulate settings into which they could fit. They simply made efforts to be with one another. Their courtship, they reminded one another, was born on Court Avenue. And whether it was infatuation or the elusive condition known as love, did not matter.

Alternating between his and her apartment in downtown Des Moines, they agreed that each place was occupied only half the time and that living in the same quarters not only would be more convenient, but also would save them money. They would stay at Samantha's. It was closer to the bus stop which would take her to the law firm for which she had just become a full-time legal aid and him to the insurance company in which he was a loan officer.

In evenings and on weekends, when they were not together in bed, Daniel and Samantha would stroll through the Papa John Sculpture Garden or participate in the night life of jazz or go into one of the hundreds of restaurants which made Des Moines a paradise for foodies. Not doubting that Samantha would say, "Yes," Daniel dropped to his knees after they returned from a concert at the Civic Center, and asked, "Will you marry me?" He was surprised by her hesitation.

"There is something you need to know about me."

"What? You've been married before?" He waited.

Samantha began, "It's complex. Are you familiar with the name *Jack Schwinder*?"

"It sounds vaguely familiar," Daniel answered. "Who is he?"

"He was a farmer. He lived south of Des Moines. We met at the law firm. He was there for some legal documents associated with the land he had bought. He called me a few days later and asked me to meet him for lunch at Smitty's, you know, the place that makes those huge pork tenderloin sandwiches? Turned out that he wasn't interested in anything related to pork or law. He was interested in me. We started seeing one another. It was easy for me, because I was working only part-time then, and it was easy for him, because there were days that he wasn't working in the fields. We spent a lot of time at his house. I didn't like being there when the weather was colder. There were mice everywhere, and I even helped him spread poison around the house."

"Your relationship must have lasted a long time," Daniel interjected.

"Over a year. But Jack was married and had two girls in elementary school. After his girls got on the bus and his wife left for work, he could do whatever pleased him until around four in the afternoon. That's when the girls got home. It was after five that he saw his wife."

Daniel appeared puzzled. "So, you regret having an affair with him?"

"He repeatedly told me that his wife didn't respect him and that he planned to ask her for a divorce. He told me how much more exciting I was. He would invite me for *Coffee with sugar*, which would signify that we would have sex. *Coffee* meant that we would just visit."

On one afternoon at his house, he told me that he couldn't divorce his wife, mainly because of his two daughters. I was furious. He betrayed me.

"Stop a while," said Daniel. "He betrayed *you*? What about his wife?"

"I didn't even know his wife. I felt so used. Jack refused to talk about it, and, without even finishing his coffee, he said he was going outside to plant mouse poison around the house. I followed him out the door, and while he dropped those grey granules of poison in certain places, I was in his face, demanding an explanation. I even placed my hand under the carton to collect some poison, so that I also could be a killer of mice. I hated them more than ever. That's when Jack thought it would be a good time for me to leave. I had to wash my hands, though, before I left, and on the way to the bathroom, I rubbed my hands together over his cup of coffee, so that some of the grains would mix with it. I hoped he would get as sick as I felt. That was the last time I ever saw him."

"So, you got some satisfaction over making him sick?" inquired Daniel.

"No, not at all," Samantha lamented. "The next week it was all over the newspapers and television that he died from the mouse poison." She began sobbing.

"Yeah, that's how I heard the name."

Samantha continued, "Someone was with him. There were two coffee cups. Police still are looking for the person who was there. That was four years ago, and the case remains open. Dan, I would never want to hurt anyone badly. I didn't mean to kill him. I've felt so guilty. You're the only one I talked about it, and I feel a little better just getting it out of my system."

Daniel was stunned. It was nearly eleven O'clock when they had returned from the concert, and he was overcome with fatigue, partially due to the late evening, but mainly a result of being broadsided by Samantha's revelations. Without speaking, he shuffled to the bedroom, undressed, and slipped under the blanket.

It was sunny when Daniel awoke, and Samantha lay next to him. He turned toward her to find that she, too, was awake. Now it was his turn for discourse. "Sam," he said quietly, "People do things they later regret. We all make mistakes, and I don't think one of them, especially one made by someone different from what she was years ago, should define that person for the rest of her life." There was a pause, and then he concluded, "I'm still with you."

"Yes, Dan," she responded to his question last night whether she would marry him. They embraced. They made love. They lay in bed. Then they selected a wedding date.

Six years into their marriage, Daniel and Samantha Goodwin were devoted to one another. He learned from his parents that they kiss when they wake up, kiss when they leave the apartment, kiss when they return home, and kiss for no reason at all.

Although their priorities always were each other, it was important that they continue the social interactions outside the marriage. They attempted, though, to minimize the hours they would spend apart. For example, when Samantha went out with her friends, Daniel would plan similar outings with his.

Despite their shared experiences, they valued privacy, and neither would ever think about opening the other's mail or even consider reviewing one another's phone. It was an unadulterated trust which forged that bond.

As the responsibilities within their careers increased, however, so did the length of time they were apart. Daniel, responsible for approving loans, was working ten-hour days, and Samantha was accompanying her attorneys on overnight business trips. But it was not only business which prevented them from being together. It was also their social lives. She was leaving their apartment more frequently to meet friends, and the evening which Daniel vividly recalls is the one in which Samantha did not kiss him when she left.

It was Daniel's birthday when only the two of them were celebrating at the Cosi Cucina restaurant. Samantha received a text message, read it, and returned the phone to her purse. The simple act of looking at the phone, to Daniel, was an interruption, a barrier to effective communication. It was allowing an uninvited individual to join them. But he said nothing about it. Neither did Samantha.

They returned to their apartment, and Samantha set her purse on the counter before going into the bathroom. Her phone sat on the top of gloves, and Daniel philosophized that, by her permitting a third party to join them during dinner, he had the right to be part of any conversation that included that unknown individual. He picked up the phone and looked for messages. There it was: *on this night I miss u more than ever. Love, E.* The text was from the law firm which employed Samantha. Edwin was the lawyer with whom she had gone to St. Louis. He was married and had three children.

Samantha returned from the bathroom, and a devastated Daniel confronted her with the message.

A divorce was in the future. In the meantime, they shared the apartment, but not the bed, and went to and from work as they always had.

The travesty of the affair consumed Daniel. *How could she do this? She violated our most sacred vows. She lied to me. I had trusted her every move. While I worshipped our relationship, she was unfaithful. I am a cuckhold.*

Samantha left for work. Daniel picked up his phone.

When Saman that arrived at the law office, two police officers met her. "Samantha Goodwin?" one of the officers asked.

"Yes," Samantha answered.

"I'm Detective Steve Wilson. You are under arrest for the murder of Jack Schwinder. You have the right to remain silent. Anything you say can be used against you in court."

Officer Flores handcuffed her.

Detective Wilson continued, "You have the right to talk to a lawyer for advice before we ask you any questions. You have the right to have a lawyer with you during questioning. If you cannot afford a lawyer, one will be appointed for you before any questioning if you wish. If you decide to answer questions now without a lawyer present, you have the right to stop answering at any time."

"Ed? This is Dan. Sam won't be in today."

Sixth Sens

Evan could read minds from the instant he was born, but he did not understand any of it at that time. He knew, for example, that his mother and father, the ones who cared for him, loved him, and that occasionally they were displeased, usually when they changed his diapers. It was only later, as he acquired language skills, that he could articulate meanings.

The friends with whom Evan played as a preschooler usually were naively honest. There were times, though, that a child would say, "My mom is calling," when Evan heard, *I have to go potty*. The difference between the comment and the intention was how Evan learned that he possessed the ability to read minds. He, himself, always was entirely honest, because he had assumed that everyone else also could read minds.

Determining what someone was thinking was possible only when the individual was in close proximity to him. In addition, he or she had to be concentrating in some way on Evan. Sheila, a neighbor who was in the same Fourth Grade class, asked, "Do you want to come over to my house?"

Normally Evan would say, "No," for fear that the other boys in his class would later tease him, but he read, *I'm helping my mom make cookies.* "Okay."

It was the following year, however, that Eddie, the meanest kid in Fifth Grade, invited Evan to his birthday party for the following Saturday afternoon. *My mom said I had to invite everyone or no one at all.*

"I can't," Evan told him. He was learning how to lie.

By the time he was in junior high school, Evan began taking advantage of his unusual capabilities. As most of the boys congregated on one side of the auditorium used for the junior-high dance, and the girls remained on the opposite side, Evan eased his way toward Abby. He had been watching her since the beginning of school and liked the way her pony tail moved when she walked. And he thought she was cute. Suddenly he read, *I wish Evan would ask me to dance.*

"Hi, Abby. Wanna dance?"

In high school, Evan realized how powerful mind reading could be, particularly when he earned his driver's license. "Dad, could I use the car for a while tonight?"

"Where are you going?"

"To the school for Science Club."

I wonder if Evan will pick up friends and drive around after leaving the school.

"I'm meeting Martin at the lab. I'll come directly home afterward."

And Evan was becoming skilled with the proper use of mind reading in the classroom. When a teacher asked him a question, he knew exactly what answer the instructor wanted. It was not as though he would earn an A in every class, though, because mind reading did not work well for written tests.

In high school he looked at Abby, whose brain said, *I think he's cute*, and Evan invited her to go to a movie with him. When the movie ended, he asked, "What would you like to do now?"

I'd like to go to Village Inn for coffee and cheesecake. "I don't know. You choose," she answered.

"How about going to Village Inn? We could have cheesecake with some coffee." Evan knew exactly what to say.

During the approximately eighteen years from Evan's birth until his graduation from high school, he honed his mind-reading skills to give himself an advantage in socializing with girls, academics, dealing with his parents, and games. He always won a hand of poker, and he seldom lost a game of chess. The real test, however, would come when he no longer was surrounded by those with whom he had grown up. It would be college.

Evan was convinced that the greatest benefits from his adeptness in determining the thoughts of others were not related to friends he had made within his dormitory, nor with the professors. They were with the young women who also studied at the university. As he walked briskly from one class to another on the sidewalks which crisscrossed the campus, he could detect some of the names of girls who passed him. Red-headed Bonnie was looking forward to a date that evening. The girl in jeans and a denim jacket had her period. A full-bodied one in a long dress liked what she saw in Evan. And a young woman—her name was Shelley—was distraught over her test grade which had just been posted.

Mind reading was the most efficient way to interact with women. There was no pretense. Evan easily found those who would like to know him, and he concentrated on the ones which he, too, may like.

It was in the end of the week of the fall semester, the weather warmed by the fading summer, when Evan met Madeline. She told him that she was a sophomore and lived off campus in a room she rented from a retired couple, but he knew those things. She thought, *Is Evan athletic? What does he do for fun? I wonder what he's like in bed.*

His face briefly reddening, Evan told her that he enjoyed running. "But I'm not part of the track team," he said. "I like to run a few miles in the morning, then shower and have breakfast. How about you?"

"I like to swim. I do it all summer long."

I know.

"That's great. Where do you swim?"

"I'm from northern Minnesota. My parents have a cabin on a lake."

I know. "That must be relaxing."

"Oh, it is. The best part is taking a sauna in the evening."

I know. And after leaving the sauna, jumping nude into the lake. "I'd like that."

"Maybe you could visit with us there sometime," Madeline said insincerely.

He brushed off what appeared an ingenuine invitation, but it would not prevent him from accepting her suggestion that they go to her apartment, where they would be able to talk further and privately. Her room was on the second floor of a house only blocks from the south side of the campus. In it were a desk, computer, miniature refrigerator, and a full bed. The bathroom, across the hall, she shared with a young woman in an adjacent room. "Where do you eat?" he asked her.

"In the Commons," she answered, "but I keep snacks and beverages in here." She pointed to the refrigerator and opened it. A bottle of vodka and a bottle of gin lay on their sides at the top, where ice cube trays normally would be. "Would you like a drink?" Madeline suggested.

Madeline poured herself a glass of vodka and poured another, a glass of gin, for Evan. They sipped their drinks, and then she said, "My hands are cold, but it's a better way to drink than to have your liquor diluted by ice cubes."

Evan held Madeline's hand in his. "I'll warm them." He then held both hands. Then they embraced and kissed. They sipped more, and Even could feel the burning as the ice-cold gin coated his throat. He read a similar feeling in Madeline. He also read that Madeline wanted him in bed, and soon they were undressing.

"That was heaven," he said to Madeline as their heavy breathing subsided. Evan read that she also enjoyed sex with him, *but who is this "Joseph"* who appeared in her head? The two of them dressed, thanked one another for the adventurous afternoon, and mentioned a possibility of meeting some other time. He left the apartment, however, with an uneasy sense that there would not be some other time.

Evan returned to his dorm to study statistical methods for the next class, Monday; he must, there was no way that his mind-reading prowess could solve theories in statistics. There would be other *Madelines* in his life. No, he had to forget Madeline. He would never compare a relationship with the fling he had just experienced.

After the Friday statistics class, Evan returned to his dormitory room and went to his computer to begin the stat assignment and thought, *Why? It's due Monday. Is there any good reason that I shouldn't enjoy the beginning of a weekend? And Horatio's has two-for-one beers every Friday evening.*

The first individual he encountered at Horatio's was a fellow student in the statistical methods class. He did not know the guy's name and could learn little about him via mind reading. Evan discovered that it was difficult to discern thoughts of someone who had consumed alcohol. There tended to be inconsistencies in thought processes and rapid changes of subjects and moods. Evan could recognize only that the student was despondent. "Rough class today, huh?" Evan remarked.

"For sure," said the student. "I'm Joe. Pull up a seat."

"Thanks. I'm Evan." They discussed some of the challenges with the course in which they were enrolled. They shared with one another their majors, the high schools from which they had come, and a little about their families. They talked about the women students, how they seemed to be more aloof, and eventually about their own exploits. "I know this sounds corny, but I thought I'd found someone who could be my soul mate. Turns out she was interested in nothing more than a one-night stand."

"Well," answered Joe, "I *did* find my soul mate. We'd been together for over a year. I couldn't get hold of her Wednesday, so I asked her what she was doing. She made up something about being with her girlfriends at the student union. That's one of the places I went. I didn't see her there. She finally admitted that she was with some guy. I'm upset, first because she lied. Second, maybe she screwed this guy. I don't know what to do."

What if we are talking about the same girl? Is Joe "Joseph?" I never imagined that it could come to this. I can't be a friend to someone whose girlfriend I fucked. And Joe, he read, *had the same thought.*

Joe continued, "What's your would-be girlfriend's name?"

Evan paused. "Shelly," he lied. After their confabulation at Horatio's, Evan and Joe saw one another only in class.

Evan passed the Statistical Methods class, barely, and he graduated with a Bachelor of Arts degree from the College of Arts and Sciences. During one of his cross-campus treks before graduation, he became fixated on a man walking toward him with Madeline next to him. The two were holding hands. He was Joseph.

Evan eventually married Abby. The marriage ended after seven years, the result of her often fantasizing about other men when the two of them had sex.

Would I be better off with or without knowing what others think? he asked himself. *If I hadn't known that Abby thought about other partners during sex, maybe we'd still be together. What I don't know wouldn't hurt me.*

Extrasensory perception is indistinguishable from the omniscience characteristic of the writer. I am Evan.

Cloistered Consequences

His family name was Stoltzfus, part of the Amish community which settled in Iowa during the mid-nineteenth century. Hard-working, religious, and family-oriented, they were a cooperative people who maintained close friendships with the other communal Amish. They also rejected the modern conveniences of technology.

But the Stoltzfuses also were among the Mennonites, who broke from the Amish, because they wanted technology to make life easier in every possible way. So, Jacob Stoltzfus, six generations later, represented the best of both ethnic groups. Just ask Keva, whom he married.

A contrast to the Amish, Keva Weber did not care whether others could see her knees. She would never wear a bonnet. She would drive her automobile. She would walk next to her husband, not behind him, and, should Keva disagree with Jacob, she would let him know. She had a disdain for patriarchs.

She said, "I do," but did not use only her husband's name. She became Keva Weber-Stoltzfus. It puzzled the Amish, even several months later.

Jacob and Keva lived in a rural area among the Amish in Johnson County, Iowa. "We don't want to be in a crowd of people," Jacob told her in reference to Iowa City. The refurbished school house which they rented was on the east side of a gravel road, which separated those who used electricity, telephones, and gasoline engines from those who did not. It was a Kalona address. It was isolated.

Keva did enjoy the quaint stores of Kalona. All the goods were made locally, and customers were treated as family.

If it were not for Keva's job at the University of Iowa Hospitals and Clinics, though, socializing would have been nearly nonexistent, and she was eager to get to work each day, but mindful that there could be horse-drawn buggies on the same road into Iowa City.

The communication and cooperation within her Infectious Diseases department created an *esprit de corps* which she found invigorating enough that she would not hesitate to work late when it benefited the hospital. In fact, as Christmas approached, Keva consented to work overtime, so that she could earn additional money to buy a watch which she wanted to get for Jacob.

Keva's daily drive from Iowa City to her rural home gave her time to reflect on her relationship with Jacob. *He had been considerate*, she thought, *particularly before we were married. He has only a part-time job hauling trash, a job that doesn't pay much, so our income is mostly from me. Once he gets an education, though, that should change. The conversation last night was what was strange. He suggested that we would have more money if I handed over my paycheck and let him pay the rent and buy the groceries.*

She could see light from the bedroom as she turned into the driveway. As she walked to the front door, she noted the kerosene-lit homes on the other side of the road.

Keva entered the kitchen and turned on the light. She had used so much time thinking about Jacob that she neglected to plan dinner. She would find something, though. She always did.

Jacob entered. "What's for supper?"

"I have some pasta. I thought I'd make a cheese sauce for it."

Staring at her for a moment, Jacob said nothing and then went to the living room and turned on the television. While the water was boiling and Keva was preparing a sauce, Jacob re-entered the kitchen, grabbed a bottle of beer from the refrigerator, and took it to the chair in front of the television.

"Dinner's ready," Keva announced at last, but Jacob remained in the living room to finish watching a sports channel. "What happened to the wine I left in the fridge from last night?" she asked.

"I drank the rest of it," he answered.

I really would have liked that glass of wine, she thought.

Jacob sat at their kitchen table, helped himself to most of the pasta and sauce, and began eating. As Keva sat, he remarked, "This sauce could use something, I don't know what." She did not answer. When he finished his pasta, he returned to the television.

After Keva cleared the table and washed the dishes and flatware, she joined Jacobin the living room. He began explaining why he thought Bob Stoops should have been hired as the Hawkeyes' coach after Hayden Frye, rather than Kirk Ferentz.

"Well, what do you think?"

She was not interested in the subject. "Maybe you're right."

Keva could not remember when it all started. She thought it began when Jacob shoved her one night after dinner. Perhaps it was even earlier, when he criticized her for her choice of clothing. She had gained a little weight during the winter, and Jacob reminded her regularly.

Whether there was too little income, an empty tank of gas, or the wrong choice of food, it was always Keva's fault, and she had to be punished. Jacob broke her glass case, the one which held the uncirculated silver dollar which her grandparents had given her with the year of her birth on it. He threw the watch which Keva had given him for Christmas onto their concrete steps and crushed it with his boot, explaining, "I wish you hadn't made me do that." He burned photographs of her family.

Jacob began turning his hostility directly onto Keva. "This is your day to die, bitch," and hit her with his fist. If she were scheduled to work the following morning, she sometimes called in to say she was sick. Otherwise, a weekend gave her enough time to hide a black eye.

The beatings, which she apparently deserved, resulted in a broken rib, the loss of teeth, and unconsciousness, but, through it all, Jacob professed his deep love for Keva. In fact, he convinced her that he was the only one—not her parents, not her grandparents, not her brothers—who really loved her.

I wonder what kind of mood Jacob's in today, was Keva's thought each time she entered their home.

It was not until her mother-in-law found her bruised and bloodied on the kitchen floor that anyone became aware of Keva's injuries. Not knowing that the perpetrator was her own son, she called the police.

Iowa City police issued a warrant for Jacob's arrest, but he fled to neighboring Nebraska, found a job in park maintenance, and stayed for six months. He also found a girlfriend who eventually called police when she was physically harmed, and Jacob returned to Iowa to face the charge of domestic abuse.

The safest Keva had felt since her marriage was when Jacob was in jail. She seemed to have forgotten the joys of freedom, and she tested her new liberty by going to the Kalona cheese shop. The owner was behind the counter. "Good morning, Mr. Lapp," she said cheerfully.

Mr. Lapp did not respond. There was no acknowledgement that she had even entered his store. Keva gazed at the other customers, mostly men, who turned their eyes from her. They all knew. She had sinned by turning on her husband. They chatted briefly with one another in hushed voices. A customer paid for a loaf of bread, and Mr. Lapp smiled, knowing that he lived in a supportive community which protected all of them.

Victim

The news story in the *Iowa* section of the Des Moines *Register* said it all: "One Killed, One Critical in Single-car Crash," an automobile accident which changed the lives of two families forever.

A late afternoon car accident took the life of one girl and left the other in critical condition Saturday afternoon on Des Moines Southside. Pronounced dead at the scene was seventeen-year-old Molly Bancroft. Transported to a local hospital was sixteen-year-old Karen Berkowitz.

Molly was the daughter of Steven and Sharon Bancroft of West Des Moines.

Karen is the daughter of Willard and Amy Berkowitz, West Des Moines. Both were juniors at Valley High School.

The crash remains under investigation.

The Bancroft and Berkowitz families maintained a cordial relationship as a result of the deep friendship their daughters shared. Willard and Amy treated Molly as though she were Karen's sister, and Karen may as well have been part of Sharon's and Steven's family. The girls were at one another's home every weekend.

The largest high school in the state of Iowa, Valley had excelled in scholastic achievement, athletics, and the arts. Its reputation, though, included vanity, and competition especially among girls reached a point at which one who was caught wearing the same clothing twice in a month was considered sub-dignified.

Karen and Molly had the solution. They wore one another's outfits at will. In effect, they doubled their wardrobes, and their families did laundry without knowing whose clothes they were. The two shared everything reasonably sensible.

The automobile was Karen's. It was the one she fantasized owning every morning that her father drove past the dealership to take her to Valley High School. It was a Porsche 718, a convertible with an electronic top. Willard told her that he would pay half the cost of the car of her choice, "But you'll be responsible for licensing and insurance."

A year after she earned her license to drive, Karen had saved enough money to pay for fifty percent of the car. It had been previously owned, but well-maintained. A two-seater, it would be the envy of the Valley boys. And Willard approved of its two seats. He had read that each additional passenger increased the probability of an accident exponentially. Limiting passengers to only one, then, would provide extra safety.

Karen quickly became adept with its six-speed manual transmission, and drove to the Bancroft's to take Molly for a ride. While waiting for Molly to come out, Karen lowered the top.

"Take a look at those tire marks," the detective said to the police officers who had responded. "They leave the road nearly a hundred yards before hitting that approach. Most of the driving was in the ditch."

"In order for the vehicle to have jumped over the approach," one officer replied, "It had to've been going at a high rate of speed, say fifty, sixty?"

"What's the speed limit? Thirty-five?" asked the detective.

The bodies were outside the Porsche, one slumped over the hood, the other tangled in a barbed wire fence. Identification was nearly impossible. Glass and metal had erased facial recognition, and the families sorted through the menagerie of rings, bracelets, makeup, and notes which each girl was known to have kept. Sharon and Steven heard the announcement they dreaded. They had lost Molly.

Autopsies are routinely completed in cases of death from vehicle crashes, and the toxicology agency of the Bureau of Environmental Health found no trace of alcohol or any chemical known to impair driving.

"Who was driving the Porsche?" That is the question which Karen's insurance company wanted to know. It was also what both the Bancrofts and the Berkowitzes desired to learn. Each couple possessed a subtle need to be able to conclude, *Our daughter was not responsible for this tragedy.*

"Karen would never knowingly go over the speed limit," Willard said to Amy, "So, she must have let Molly drive her car."

"It was Karen's car. She just bought it. Why would she let Molly drive it so soon?"

Sharon asked Steven.

Steve responded, "I don't know if Molly even knew how to drive a stick."

It was a closed-casket funeral for Molly. Among her classmates and relatives were Willard and Amy, who expressed their condolences and, when asked about Karen, indicated that she remained in a coma at Methodist Hospital in Des Moines.

Crises often brings people together via a twisted type of *esprit de corps*, but this accident, which left one family with a burial and another with a child in intensive care, would first require acceptance and then forgiveness.

The Bancrofts went daily to the Resthaven Cemetery to visit Molly. There were no visible headstones. Each grave was marked with a plaque grounded where a head stone normally would be. On Molly's plaque, they placed daisies, her favorite.

The Berkowitzes visited the comatose Karen every day at the Iowa Methodist Medical Center. Despite her feeding tubes and still-bandaged face, they never lost their hope that someday she would suddenly regain consciousness, yet they existed in an aura of fear that a phone call from the hospital would report that her revival is futile.

It had been a month since the accident. The Bancrofts remained in mourning, and the Berkowitzes' anxieties persisted. Willard's phone rang. His hands shook as he listened to a nurse introduce herself from Methodist Hospital. "Karen," she told him, "...is responding to stimuli. We're hopeful that she will be alert soon."

Amy and Willard immediately left their West Des Moines home for Methodist Hospital. Had they turned off the lights? They did not care. They were going to see Karen. She would live.

Willard and Amy were at Karen's hospital bed for over an hour before they detected any form of movement. Her head turned ever so slightly, and they approached her. While Willard held her hand, Amy massaged her forehead. "Honey, it's Mom and Dad."

The daughter's eyes fluttered. She opened and closed them. She opened them again and spoke, "Amy… Willard… Where's Karen?"

Game

I realized the moment I saw Sophia that I wanted to know her. We worked on the same floor of the eight-story Exchange Building, but on opposite sides. We were on our computers all day. She stared at one monitor and entered data. I needed three monitors for all the programs I used. I could look to my left for a side-view of her. Sometimes, I would notice her peering at me, and Sophia would quickly turn her head back to her screen.

Figuratively, we were predisposed to play a game of chess.

I found work-related reasons to venture to her area, so that I could say, "Hi," or "Good morning," or "That was some storm last night, wasn't it?" That's the way all relationships or friendships start; with neutral or at least non-controversial comments. You begin saying things which suggest that you are part of that other person's beliefs. You have something in common. Some call it *small talk*.

Small talk is part of what pawns do. They are not too powerful, but nevertheless important in chess. Pawns protect the other aspects of our character. We can lose pawns and still manage to win the game, but if you lose too many of them, you risk the loss of more important pieces which the pawns guard. Pawns go only forward, one or two steps on the first move and, after that, only one square at a time. The sole time that a pawn may capture another piece is when the opponent is one square in front and to the side of it. In our chess game I made the first move by taking my king's pawn two steps forward.

Sophia responded with, "Hello. How are you?" but she appeared guarded. She also moved her king's pawn two steps ahead.

"I'm Tony," I said.

"I'm Sophia," she answered. Neither of us had to give our name. The other already knew it.

Now I could move my queen. Queens are the most powerful pieces on the board, and each player has only one. They can move as far as they want in a straight line, but they cannot jump over other pieces. I moved my queen diagonally, just in front of my bishop's pawn F. I like to have clear paths, so that I can dominate the center, but I don't like placing my queen too far in front; she's a target for every opponent. We all have the strengths of queens, but, without the protection of mostly bishops, knights, and rooks, they can be vulnerable.

Sophia was moving the same pieces I had, but not exactly in the identical places. She allowed me to sit with her during a thirty-minute lunch.

Because the Exchange Building was filled with the art in which its founder had invested, our conversation easily turned to paintings and sculptures, and I learned that Sophia enjoyed visits to art museums as much as I did. Our first *date*, then, was to the Metropolitan Museum of Art. Bishops move in straight lines on their own colors. They are like most of us: staying with our own cultures, religions, and politics. Sophia's bishop and mine were on the same color, and I moved in to take hers.

Rooks also go in straight lines, but only forward or to the side. Our rigidity resembles that of rooks. At the art museum Sophia professed a profound fondness for impressionism, but was not willing even to discuss possible merits of abstract expressionism. I moved my rook, so that the only piece sitting between it and herking was a pawn.

Our game was on: we began having dinners together, and I was charmed by her sincerity, attentiveness, and patience. I was entirely bewildered, though, by her avoiding talking about her family. The most I could learn was that she was an only child reared most of her life by her mother. Some things in life do not have to be addressed immediately, it seems. We can confront them later. Knights are the only pieces which can jump over others, and they move two ahead and one to the side or one ahead and two to the side. I left her pieces on the board and jumped over them with my knight, landing closer to her king.

I have waited long enough to describe the king. The queen may be the most powerful player, but it is the king which opponents need to reach. It is how the game is won. It can move only one square at a time. The king can never be captured, only checked by opposing pieces. For example, any other player on the board in line with a bishop can be taken by that bishop. Not the king, though. Rules prevent him from being in line with it or even occupying a square on which an opposite player threatens. And when the king is unable to move to an unguarded position, it is the end of the game, Checkmate.

The king is our ego. We guard it with all our strength, our environment, and our friends. On the chess board the king is so important that we advance our bishops, rooks, and knights cautiously, so that he remains safe.

Chess matches can be lengthy, especially when they involve romance, Every moment that I was with Sophia, sometimes at my apartment and often at hers, she became more attractive to me. And as much as I wanted to hold and caress her, I opted, instead, to wait for the right time, something which would come more quickly without my being aggressive.

The frequency with which Sophia and I were together allowed me to discover that what I first had assumed was aloofness was actually a fear of being abandoned, maybe not even physically, but emotionally. Her father had left her and her mother when she was only four years old, and she apparently was unable to develop trust in any male figure.

"The last thing I remember him saying," she told me when we were at her place, "…was, 'I'll always be with you,' and I waited every night for him to come to me until it became simply a bad memory." At that point we were beyond the use of pawns, and we had used our rooks, bishops, and knights to their full extent. Now our kings and queens were most important to us, and I hugged Sophia. She responded by embracing me more tightly. We held one another, pressing from the chests to pelvic areas. And then we kissed mouth-to-mouth and moved to the bed.

Undressed, Sophia displayed exactly what I could feel through her clothing, and, following what probably was some fumbling foreplay, there was penetration. I had captured her queen.

I needed only to use my queen to take the pawn directly in front of the king. Her king could not take my queen, because that space was guarded by my knight. In one move it would be checkmate.

I couldn't do it. An ego is fragile. Instead, I moved my queen to block a pawn, the only move which Sophia had left. Now the only piece available was her king, which was not in check. The only place it could move, though, was one space ahead, the square guarded by my knight. Rules of chess do not allow a king to move into *check*. If it currently is not in check, but cannot move without being in check, there is no winner. It is a stalemate.

Now this is not part of the rules of chess: it may be more appropriate to proclaim in a stalemate not that there is no winner, but that both are winners. Sometimes by not winning, you win.

On the Air with Julio

The three girls were at home in Marla's bedroom for a sleepover. A radio was tuned to KLMB. They were waiting for "On the Air with Julio," the talk show which friends Sonja and Alda felt attracted the most pathetic callers in the city, and they seldom missed its introduction, *YOU'RE ON THE AIR WITH HOO LEE OH*. Freshmen in high school, they usually found some venue every Friday evening to listen to advice for cheating husbands, abusive boyfriends, and pregnant teenagers. If they did not learn how the maladies could affect their own behavior, they at least had subjects which they could criticize.

Precisely at nine o'clock they heard, *You're on the air with Julio. Our first caller is Jeff. What's happening, Jeff?*

It's my girlfriend. We've been going together for four months, and I just found out that she had a baby over a year ago and gave it up for adoption. Why didn't she tell me?

Are you serious about this young woman?

Well, I was.

Listen Jeff, maybe it just wasn't the right time. Four months is not a long time. If she is as serious about you as you are about her, she would disclose it to you in due time.

And remember: neither of you has to know everything in one another's past. Thank you for calling.

"What's wrong with Jeff, anyway?" Sonja asked. "Was he looking for a virgin?"

Alda answered, "Maybe he wanted to be the first father for his girlfriend."

Receptionist Margaret screened all the calls for Julio, just as she had done for countless other talk-show hosts over the years. *Keep those calls coming. Dial 555-KLMB. Our next call is from Lisa. Hi, Lisa. You're on the air. Thank you for calling. What's going on in your life?*

My boyfriend Rob and I have been together for two years. I love him to death, but every time we argue, he stays away from me for days and usually goes out with someone else.

Do you live together?

No, but we're in a relationship. We've talked about marriage.

Don't you think that Rob should stop running away from problems? If he sees someone else every time he disagrees with you, what makes you think that he won't do that, once you are married? Tell him to stay with the other woman. Say, 'Good-bye, Rob.' Good luck Lisa.

"Good-bye, Rob," the three of them said almost in unison.

Sonja suddenly looked as though she were ready to applaud. "We should call Julio."

"What would we say?" asked Alda.

"Anything," Sonja answered. "We'll think of something. Let's have some fun."

Marla interjected, "I know. We can say we're committing suicide. We'll see what kind of advice he has for us."

"But," Alda emphasized. "Only one of us calls him. I think it should be Marla. She thought of it first. Besides, Marla can be more serious."

Marla consented, "On two conditions. I'm not going to use my real name, because someone might be able to tell who I am. Also, don't either one of you make noise or laugh while I'm doing it. Give me a name."

Alda whispered in Sonja's ear.

Sonja thought and then whispered in the ear of Alda.

Alda announced, "Nora. Nora will be your name." Nora was the name of a bullied girl in some of their classes.

Ladies and gentlemen, we have Nora on the line. Thank you for calling, Nora. What's on your mind?

"Suicide," said Marla. "*Suicide*," said Nora.

There was a pause on the radio. *What is troubling you?*

I'm alone. No one likes me. I have no friends. I'm not invited anywhere. This is the end. Good-bye. The connection between Marla and KLMB radio was broken, and the girls giggled as the station went to a commercial break.

A minute later Julio was back. *If you're listening, Nora, please understand that there are better options for you.*

"Oh, pleeeeze," Marla implored. "Leave it alone. Take a call from someone else."

Julio persisted. *Nora, you are loved. Please call back. There is help. There's a hot line, a number you can call. It is one eight hundred, two seven three, three two five five. Twenty-four hours a day. If you don't want to call me, call that hot line.*

Alda remarked, "He seems to be a bit bothered by Marla's call."

"Nora's call," Marla corrected her.

Nora, I can tell that you are a beautiful girl, inside and out, and the world will be worse off without you. It seems that sometimes the pain can be so great that the easiest way to get rid of it is to end your life, but there are some better ways to erase the pain.

"Marla, don't you think this is getting a little boring?" Sonja asked.

"You want me to call him to say it was all a joke?" she answered sarcastically.

"Maybe you should."

Julio continued. *Nora, if you're listening, think about this for a moment: Ending your life is a permanent solution to a temporary problem. No one wants that.*

Margaret took the call from Marla. "This is Nora, not my real name. I'm the one who called about suicide. It was a joke. I'm sorry."

"I've never felt so humiliated," Julio replied to Margaret when she told him about the call after the show ended. "Do kids have nothing better to do?"

"I wouldn't worry about it, Julio," Margaret assured him. "That's the advantage of radio. You never see your audience, and your audience never sees you. Imagination is important. It's what makes radio a magic medium. Nora may not have been serious, but your audience doesn't know that. Forget about it. Next Friday will be an entirely new show."

The show which Julio had finished seemed a calamity, but the seven days which intervened restored his confidence, and he was prepared for anything the following Friday.

YOU'RE ON THE AIR WITH HOO LEE OH. Our first caller is John. John, how can I help you? John was home for the weekend from college and soon would be home for the summer, and his parents were nagging him to find a job.

Peggy asked Julio for suggestions for confronting her boyfriend concerning his poor etiquette, and Joseph wanted to know how he could find whether his fiancé had been cheating on him. The show was going well, and Julio dispensed answers with precision.

We have time for one more call. On the line with me is, Julio hesitated. Hadn't he told Margaret not to accept a call from her? *Nora. Nora, may I help you?*

The voice said, *No, you already have. Last week you were talking to a girl, also named 'Nora', about suicide. At the time I had in front of me twenty-one hydrocodone tablets and a bottle of vodka. I was ready to consume it all, but I waited to hear what you had to say. By the time you finished, I decided not to do it. Thank you.*

Falcon

Hot, dry, and dusty characterized the pow-wow, as it did every summer (*bloketu*) on the Rosebud Indian Reservation. Whirlwinds mysteriously appeared randomly across the fairgrounds, and they mocked tornadoes by spinning sand into the faces of the Lakota who were erecting teepees where they would sleep during the three-day celebration in south central South Dakota.

I traveled to Rosebud each June, a way I thought I could immerse myself in the native American culture which had existed a century and a half ago, not the society which now was obliterating its language, traditions, extended families, and self-sufficiency. I wanted to be part of the Sioux Nation, just as my Indian friends had become part, albeit neglected, of an Anglo America.

Hundreds of teepees sprang from the worthless sand and limestone prairie (*oblaye*) and, from a distance, simulated pointed party-hats with stiff tassels. From where had they all come? Signs of their existence were absent until the annual commemoration. In antiquity, they supported the way of life for a nomadic Lakota who followed the movements of bison (*tatanka*) on which they depended for food and clothing. Now they were only symbolic of an era of self-government which no longer existed.

I recognized Chayton standing near the drum which half a dozen elders would beat for the pow-wow while chanting. We had graduated Todd County High School the same year in Mission. He returned to the rez after earning a degree in sociology and made it a point to be home for the gala. He expected me also to be there. He was my link to Lakota culture. "*How*, *Kola*," I said to him.

Chayton responded, "Hello, Friend." He told me that he had little time to talk. He needed to get into his costume of moccasins, leather, and feathers. He would be dancing on the round, hard, dirt floor that evening.

"Enit," I said, because it was the response native Americans gave to acknowledge another's comment. I would watch him dance, but I knew we would not have any time together. When one begins dancing, he does not stop.

I made my way to a teepee. Half a dozen adults easily could stand inside. It consisted of several poles originating from a circle and meeting at the top. Deerskins wrapped around the poles. There were paintings of birds (*zintkala*) on the hides. I was fully aware that the teepee was the home, at least temporarily, of someone, so I had no right to enter, but I had never been inside one. Through a series of rationalizations, then, I gave myself permission to pull open the flap which covered the entrance, and I stepped into that giant cone.

I wish that somehow, I could have prepared myself for what I saw inside that teepee. I had traveled in time to the 1850s and suddenly was confronted by the present, as a tumult abruptly startles us from dreams, and, once awake, we have no idea who or where we are.

A cord ran from the outside under the deer skin. It was attached to a cart with wheels. Plugged into the electrical system was a black and white television receiver tuned into the only TV station which reached the reservation, a signal aided by a translator halfway between KELO-TV in Sioux Falls, on the eastern side of the state, and Rosebud. Sitting on top of the television set were two antennae, "rabbit ears." It did not matter that the screen resembled snow in a blizzard. It was reality. It was stark. It was traumatic. It was at a pow-wow, and I was stunned.

Chayton is the Lakota name meaning "Falcon."

We can never return.

Fire Boy

Friday evenings were goals in West Des Moines, especially for Ryan Keller, a prep cook at Fabian's Bar and Grill since graduating Dowling Catholic High School. From ten-thirty in the morning until four in the afternoon Monday through Friday he chopped onions, deveined shrimp, cut meat, and parboiled vegetables and took all their kitchen's smells back to his girlfriend's apartment. It may have been a factor in Sheila's telling him the previous night that their relationship had become foul.

Sheila commuted daily to downtown Des Moines. An employee of the state of Iowa, she entered computer data for the Department for the Blind. Her job was stable, and her income allowed her to secure her own apartment and a pre-owned automobile. Ryan contributed, but his hourly wage was low by comparison.

Summer was ending, yet it remained hot. Humidity made the heat of the kitchen worse. Ryan entered Fabian's through its back door. Fellow cook Miguel placed his hand on Ryan's shoulder. "Boss wants to see you."

"Hi, Ryan," kitchen manager Bradley started. "I'm sorry I have to do this. Food costs have become too high, so the general manager has decreased my budget. I'll have to do much of the work you were doing. It's gonna be hard on all of us. The hostess has your pay for this week at the front. Good luck."

"Screw you," Ryan whispered as he walked among tables being covered with checkered cloths. He took his pay in cash and left Fabian's to return to his—no, Sheila's—apartment. He thought about his best high school buddy, who continued his education at the community college and was now living in Denver. *Wish I'd done something after school,* he thought. Dark cumulus clouds were forming. *I don't even wanna be here*, he declared to himself as he walked into the place Sheila had shared with him during the last three months. *I'm tired of that girl. I'm going to Denver.*

Ryan found the duffle bag he had stashed in the closet of the master bedroom. Yes, the knife with the switch blade remained inside it. He was convinced that the knife once saved his life. As a hitchhiker, he had been offered a ride by an over-the-road truck driver, who, after an hour on the interstate, pulled onto the shoulder and demanded a sexual act. That's when Ryan pulled out the knife and kept it trained on the driver until he had driven into the next city to let him off. If he were to get to Denver, he may need his knife again.

He pulled open drawers to find all the clothing he would need during the following several days and then scoured the bathroom for his tooth brush and paste, antiperspirant, and hair brush. He took a bar of soap and a towel and returned to the bedroom for a pair of shoes. He opened a drawer again, this time one of Sheila's, and rummaged through her clothing and jewelry. Beneath her folded underwear were three crisp twenty-dollar bills. He hid them in the inside pocket of the duffle bag and, feeling defiant about not leaving any sort of note, left the complex—and Sheila—forever.

The former prep cook, periodically changing from one arm to the other to carry the duffle bag, walked south along Forty-second Street, which included a bridge over the MacVicar Freeway. He would never be able to hitch a ride on the freeway. The only things which ever slowed the sixty-miles-an-hour traffic were accidents. Ryan continued until he reached Woodland Avenue and then turned west and eventually approached a town home complex of about fifty units. Most of them were bi-attached. All of them were painted light brown with dark brown trim, and all the doors were bright red. Every one of the homes had a double garage. *Why does everyone need two cars?* he wondered.

Justification for taking someone's car, in Ryan's mind, was easy. *Those people were privileged. Any of them could manage with one car. And they must have lots of money. Anyway, I won't wreck the car. They'll get it back.*

Drops of rain began covering his bare arms, and Ryan scouted homes with lights on. One in particular appealed to him. It was on a cul-de-sac, and he could not see the front door until he walked around the east-facing garage. *Whatever happens there, no one will be able to see.*

A few steps took him to a porch. On a door mat was printed *Dave and Jude WELCOME you*. Ryan used his right hand to take the duffle bag from his left, and rang the doorbell. Lightning flashed, and a loud thunder clap followed. A middle-aged woman answered.

"Hello," Ryan began. "I'm sorry to bother you. My car broke down, and my phone died." Rain was now running through downspouts, and it was starting to get dark.

"Come in. You can use mine."

"Oh, thank you," Ryan said as he stepped onto the foyer. "My name is Joe. Something smells really good."

"I'm Jude. My husband and I just took a cake out of the oven. Tomorrow is our grandson's birthday. Pete's going to decorate it once it's cooled."

Pete? I thought it was Dave and Jude, not Pete and Jude. What kind of people would deliberately give me a false name? Ryan could not have known that, beginning at the age of ten, Dave lived on the desolate Rosebud Indian Reservation in South Dakota. Consider it the lack of facilities for recreation or a penchant he had for mischief: Dave learned that flour particles in the air can burn, so he would build small fires and throw hands full of flour through them. The results were explosive, and his Native American friends called him *Peta Hoksila*, which in the Lakota language means "Fire Boy." He, later, was simply known as Pete.

"I think it's already cool enough," Pete answered. "I just need to make some frosting." He had butter at room temperature in a bowl, and he was about to add the powdered sugar when a bolt of lightning disrupted electrical supplies.

Jude peered beyond Ryan to see that her neighbors' power also was off.

"Why don't you bring in your bag, so that it doesn't get wet?"

She saw "Ryan" written in black marker on the bag.

"Hard to say how long it'll take to get power again." Pete shrugged. "Let's use candles. Otherwise, in a half hour we probably won't be able to see anything. Joe, come on up. We can sit here in the kitchen until power returns."

Ryan took a phone from his pocket and placed it in the duffle bag. As he withdrew his hand, he removed the knife, which he slipped into his front pocket, and followed Jude up the stairs to the kitchen.

Pete had a candle burning on the counter of a center island. There were three bar stools on its north side, and Pete pulled one of them around the south side, so that he could face Jude on the right and Ryan on the left.

Ryan explained that he was from Council Bluffs and was driving to Chicago. His car, he said, broke down on the freeway.

There is something strange about Joe's story, Pete thought. *The freeway isn't accessible from Forty-second Street, so he would have to come from Fiftieth, another mile west. That's a long way to walk. And why our house?*

"Do you need one of our phones to make a call?"

"No," Ryan replied. "I don't know anyone to call. I just need your phones, both of them." He pulled the knife from his front pocket.

"What is it that you want?" asked Pete.

The reply from Ryan was, "A car. And I don't want to make it easy for you call the police." He pressed the release on the knife, and a blade swung out. He placed it close to Jude's neck.

Both Pete and Jude slid their cell phones along the counter until they were in front of Ryan. "The garage door is electric, so you can't drive the car out without power,"

Pete reminded him. *I hope he doesn't understand that the door can be disengaged from the motor*, he worried.

"Then we'll wait," was Ryan's answer.

There was silence. Anxieties were mounting, especially for Pete. Joe was threatening his wife. Light from the candle under his chin made his face appear even more sinister. Pete felt that he must resolve this problem before the restoration of power. He could not let him hurt Jude. *Peta Hoksila*, he thought. *Flour can burn. Can confectioner's sugar?* He slowly dipped his right hand into the plastic sack and spread his fingers until he could grasp enough powdered sugar to approximate the size of a baseball, and with the speed of a pitcher, threw it directly through the candle flame into the face of the unwanted guest.

The question whether powdered sugar can burn had an instant answer. There was an intense, explosive, short-lived fireball, and Jude reflexively jumped away from it as Ryan dropped the knife. The quartz countertop was unphased, but Ryan's face was not. "You, son of a bitch!" he was screaming. "What did you do to my eyes? I can't see. I'll kill you." With his arms he wiped the counter in search of the knife and swept the candle and holder against an adjacent cupboard. His rants became whimpers, and he pressed his hands against his eyes as he murmured, "You bastard."

The stench of burning flesh and scorched hair hung in the still air.

Pete finally spoke. "Jude, help me find the candle. We need some light."

Both were on their hands and knees to cover all the floor space needed to find it.

"Here it is," Jude said. It was nearly the same instant that Pete found the knife and, without announcing it, quietly placed it on the floor of the cupboard where they collected trash. Ryan was groaning.

Pete relit the candle. Ryan was face down on the countertop with his hands on his eyes. "I'm going to get a wet towel for Joe," Jude told him.

"Help me," Ryan moaned.

Jude returned with the towel and asked him to sit straight, so that she might apply it to relieve the pain. When he took his hands from his eyes, she gasped.

I have just caramelized his eyes, Pete thought.

Jude was stern. "We need to get you to a hospital." She then let him use the towel however he wanted.

"I'll call 911," offered Pete.

"No." Now, it was Ryan who was stern. He quickly calculated that police sometimes become involved when there are emergencies. "An ambulance would cost more, and I don't have insurance. You'll pay for this."

Pete realized there was no chance that Ryan would seek legal counsel for his injuries, and Ryan was certain that Pete and Jude would not file a complaint with police.

"I'll get the car ready." Pete hurried to the garage and disconnected the lever attached to the motor and manually lifted the door until its roller swallowed the door to open completely. He then backed the car onto the driveway and let it idle.

When Pete returned to the house Jude was helping Ryan to his feet. She and Pete then guided him down the steps and into the car, and they sped to MercyOne West Des Moines Hospital.

Friday evening had been exhausting, and on Saturday Pete and Jude went to a commercial bakery for a birthday cake for their grandson.

It was Sunday that Pete and Jude returned to the hospital with Ryan's duffle bag and were allowed in his room to visit. He apparently was sleeping. Bandages circled the top half of his head, and salve covered his red and black cheeks. A sign at the foot of his bed read "Keller."

Jobs consumed most of the couple's days, but on Wednesday evening the two of them found some time to return to the hospital to visit Mr. Keller. The receptionist indicated that he had been released that morning, and, following what was a cross-examination by Pete and Jude, disclosed that a vehicle from the Iowa Department for the Blind had come for him.

"I think I'd like to be known by my actual name, instead of Pete," Dave told Jude when they had returned to their home.

The knife became a souvenir of what they called "that horrendous Friday," and the newest charity to which they contributed became the American Foundation for the Blind.

Sweet Potato Pie

I knew that she would become my girlfriend. I simply did not know how long it would take. I would watch her leave her loft off Court Avenue each morning and walk the four blocks to Java Joe's, the coffee shop which she managed in downtown Des Moines.

I, too, had a loft, but I worked from home. I was a technical writer, and plumbing manufacturers and cabinet companies and flooring specialists provided ample work for me. In addition to the just compensation, I enjoyed numerous breaks, exotic vacations, and unlimited leisure. My boss was ideal; he was I.

Her name, I learned during the fourth or fifth time I went to Java Joe's, was Yamileth. Its origin, she told me, was Arabic and meant *beautiful, but strong*. I have no clue why her parents would give her an Arabic name. They were born in Georgia and always will be in Savannah. Yamileth moved to Des Moines to get away from them. Why Des Moines? She wanted a city which she felt would be the last place in the United States to which they would ever want to travel.

Java Joe's brewed an astounding number of different coffees. Its hot chocolate was rich, and it was topped with whipped cream. And the pastries were the embodiment of decadence. Its greatest gem, though, was Yamileth. I loved the name "Yamileth," because it remined me of a yam. The yam is a nearly perfect food. Its color is attractive. Its nutritional value is unparalleled. And it contains beta-carotenes and carotenoids. The only way to elevate the yam is by making it sensual, as in a pie.

Let me start, then, with Yamileth, one sweet potato I called "Sweet P." Sweet P was hot, especially with foreplay. Our relationship was one I would have described during prepubescence as "mushy," but it is the consistency necessary if I were to add something to our association, such as half a cup of butter. Flattering Sweet P, even with half a cup, was easy for me. "You have the nicest complexion," I had told her. "Your white, perfectly-aligned teeth excite me whenever you smile." And I was sincere when I complimented her. Here is the evidence that I was genuine: I had a habit, when sexually aroused, of using spoonerisms, so the first time I was able to have a conversation with Sweet P at Java Joe's, I said, "You're tun to falk with."

The pie also needs up to a cup of sugar, no problem with Sweet P, sweet, I felt, in all respects. She came prepared for Des Moines, knowledgeable as a result of the research she had done months before arriving. That's how I learned that there is only one city in the United States which has more restaurants per ten thousand residents than Des Moines has. It is San Fransisco, three times more populous. Committed to working in a service industry, specifically restaurants, Sweet P was confident, then, that she would find employment. In addition, she read that downtown Des Moines was thriving and livable and that commutes were reasonable. "Reasonable?" she asked. "I can walk to work, and I can use the bus." Any shortcomings, Sweet P discerned about Des Moines, she kept to herself, and that is what was sweet about her.

Sweet P was slim. When she picked up an order at JJ's, I watched her rear move ever-so-slightly from side to side with each step. Then she would return with my hot chocolate and baklava, and with each foot strike her firmly affixed breasts would dip. I fantasized that she wore no clothing and that she were coming from *our* kitchen. When she set the pastry and cocoa in front of me, I asked, "Would you please put a wallop of dipped cream in the cup?" We would be married, have sex before every lunch, and plan a time to have a child. Mammary glands are natural for all mammals. She would breastfeed our boy or girl. Our pie needs a half cup of milk.

When we began having sexual intercourse, we were not especially careful. Had one of us had any form of birth control, the other may have thought, *Who else benefited?* But we were fortunate. Because we were not willing to rely indefinitely upon luck, though, we began tracking her menstrual cycles, timing when the ovum would least likely travel from her Fallopian tubes to the uterus, the "rhythm method." Our pie needs two eggs.

We spiced our sexual relationship with variety. We teased. We experimented with different positions. We tried beds, chairs, and floors. And we went to diverse places. For our pie we added a big pinch of nutmeg and another of cinnamon and then mixed in a teaspoon of vanilla extract before pouring it into a premade pie crust.

Downtown Des Moines was hot. Sweet P was hot. The pie baked in a four-hundred-degree oven for about twenty minutes. When we could withdraw a clean toothpick from our dessert, it was done. Only one sexy item would be added to each slice before eating: whipped cream.

Pies cool. So do relationships sometimes. Cracks usually form on sweet potato pies, but they do not affect the taste. Cracks in alliances, though, must be mended if the association is to continue. Sweet P and I began disagreeing about things we formerly accepted, such as our commitment to one another. When I had said that I did not really want to get married, she agreed. Now, it seemed, she was looking for a permanent relationship. We had sex less frequently.

I discovered that Sweet P was sharing her pie with someone else, the one action I could not tolerate. We split. I am thankful that we did not marry. Infidelity would call for a divorce. On the other hand, maybe if we had married one another, she may have been faithful. I cannot decide whether we were not together long enough to be successful or were with one another too long without planning for a future. We never discussed cohabitation, so we retained our own lofts. Yamileth and I went our separate ways.

The pie serves more than one: that is the trouble with some recipes.

A Modern Modest Proposal

It's time we discuss the airline industry. You don't have to experience a hundred flights to realize that airlines don't give a crap about their customers. For example, I was waiting in line for a boarding pass, and the man in front of me had one carry-on bag. So did I. To be considered a carry-on, though, it had to fit into a twelve-by-fourteen-inch space. His fit, but mine was two inches too long, and I was charged an additional fifty dollars to transport it.

The guy in front of me was a big one. I mean, he had to have weighed at least three hundred fifty pounds. Compare his weight with my one hundred thirty, not much more than a third. So, I began searching for ways in which airlines could make customers' costs more equitable.

I know what you're thinking; use passengers' mass as the basis for determining prices. No, that would be unfair. Consider the couple, home at night in Cedar Rapids, Iowa. "Honey, you've hardly touched your dinner. Are you feeling all right?"

"Oh, I'm fine. It's just that I have to get a flight to Boston next week, and I thought that I probably should start fasting." Once the passengers boarded, they would all be clamoring for that ten-dollar sandwich. The plane wouldn't be able to stock enough of them.

No, my plan is much more impartial.

Consider that a gallon of jet fuel costs a dollar twenty cents. To transport one pound a distance of one hundred miles would cost an estimated five dollars. Taking that same pound to the east coast, then, would require at least fifty dollars.

Also consider that the average adult, at any given time, carries with him or her about one pound of feces. If there were a way to eliminate the stool before boarding, the savings could be tremendous. So, I have a suggestion concerning how to keep poop off the plane.

With every ticket issued would come a laxative. Every passenger would be required to be at the airport at least two hours before departure to ingest it. And who would not want to be there two hours early?

Boarding passes would be provided at restroom stalls. An Executive Excrement Examiner (EEE) would be responsible for confirming that the toilet bowl for which he or she is responsible was sufficiently full.

In the end, a thousand-mile flight with two hundred passengers would cost ten thousand dollars less. Airlines would need to be less concerned with the sizes of carry-ons. And both the three-hundred-fifty-pound and the one-hundred-thirty-pound passengers would pay the same amounts.

The first carrier to adopt my proposal could even have a marketing advantage: "Fly with Us, The Airline That Gives a Shit."

www.ingramcontent.com/pod-product-compliance
Lightning Source LLC
Chambersburg PA
CBHW050549160726
48003CB00002B/820